AF279296

*And He sat
down opposite the
treasury, and began
observing how the people
were putting money into the
treasury; and many rich people were
putting in large sums. A poor widow
came and put in two small copper
coins, which amount to a cent. Calling
His disciples to Him, He said to them,
"Truly I say to you, this poor widow
put in more than all the contributors to
the treasury; for they all put in out of
their surplus, but she, out of her
poverty, put in all she owned, all she
had to live on."*

—MARK 12:41–44, NASB

Ordinary Women of the BIBLE

✦

Ordinary Women of the BIBLE

RICH BEYOND MEASURE

ZLATA'S STORY

Robin Lee Hatcher

Ordinary Women of the BIBLE

RICH BEYOND MEASURE

ZLATA'S STORY

Dedication

To the pastors and Bible study leaders who have
fanned the flames of my love for the written
word of God throughout the years

To my CdA sisters in Christ who helped give
me the courage to step into the time of Yeshua
and experience the story for myself

Glossary of TERMS

Adonai • Lord, master; a name that implies relationship (God is Lord and we are His servants)

El Shaddai • God Almighty; the covenant name of God

The Shema • The declaration "Hear, O Israel! The Lord is our God, the Lord is one!" (Deuteronomy 6:4). "Shema" comes from the first Hebrew word of the verse, *sh'ma,* "hear." Religious Jews recite the Shema three times daily as part of their devotional life; no Sabbath worship is conducted in the synagogue without its proclamation.

soreg • a low, latticed screen or railing (in the temple complex, the soreg separated the temple courts from the Court of the Gentiles)

sudarium • a linen square placed over the face before burial

PART I

Spring, during the second year of Yeshua's Galilean ministry

Jesus was going throughout all Galilee, teaching in their synagogues and proclaiming the gospel of the kingdom, and healing every kind of disease and every kind of sickness among the people. The news about Him spread throughout all Syria; and they brought to Him all who were ill, those suffering with various diseases and pains, demoniacs, epileptics, paralytics; and He healed them. Large crowds followed Him from Galilee and the Decapolis and Jerusalem and Judea and from beyond the Jordan.

—Matthew 4:23–25, NASB

CHAPTER ONE

"Zlata. Zlata, you are needed. Come now."

Zlata groaned, trying to refuse the summons by sheer will.

Dara shook her shoulder. "Now, Zlata. The mistress needs you."

She opened her eyes at last. The room was dark except for the flickering light provided by the lamp the young servant carried. Zlata wondered how long she had been asleep. Ten minutes. An hour. However much, it had been too little.

"I'm coming, Dara." She shoved aside the light covering on her sleeping mat and sat up, hair tumbling over her shoulders as she leaned forward in search of her sandals.

Her mother-in-law's illness had cast a pall over the household for several weeks. With Abra too sick to travel to Jerusalem for Passover, Zlata's father-in-law, Taneli, had gone alone. He wasn't a patient or kind man under the best circumstances, and his wife's failing health had made him even surlier. Since his return to Capernaum, he'd spent little time at home. But that was not unusual. His obligations took him to the synagogue daily. He was an important man in the region.

It was just as well for Zlata that Taneli was wanted elsewhere for most hours of the day. He believed all women were beneath him, but he particularly detested the sight of his daughter-in-law. She understood. She reminded him of Yerik, his only son. Taneli blamed her for Yerik's death. So she did her best to remain unnoticed, a ghost within the walls of this household. But how would she avoid him in the middle of the night?

After hastily making herself presentable, she followed Dara from the room. They found Abra alone in the large sleeping chamber on the opposite side of the house, rolling her head from side to side, face beaded with sweat. She mumbled nonsensical words in a continuous stream.

Zlata knelt at the edge of the bed and took her mother-in-law's hand. Leaning close, she said, "I am here, Abra."

Her mother-in-law's fingers tightened, ever so slightly, around Zlata's hand. The two of them were not close. Like her husband, Abra scarcely gave Zlata notice. But still the woman must have drawn some comfort from her care.

Dara brought a bowl of water and a clean cloth to the bedside, and Zlata used it to cool Abra's forehead. Softly, she whispered the words of David. "In peace I will both lie down and sleep, for You alone, O Lord, make me to dwell in safety." She leaned closer. "My lady, the Lord causes you to dwell in safety. You may rest now."

Her own chest tightened as she spoke the words. They were the same ones her father had said to her mother when she lay dying. Zlata had watched from the opposite side of the bed as he'd tenderly ministered to his wife, and she'd thanked God for blessing her with devoted parents and a good, God-fearing home. By their example, she had learned what a loving marriage should look like.

Zlata had believed that her mother's death was the worst that could happen to her. How naive she'd been. How foolish. Her mother's death had not been the worst. It had only been the beginning of Zlata's losses, one piled upon another.

Zlata had been a favored child, loved and cherished by her parents. If her father had grieved over not having a son, he'd never once shown those feelings to his daughter. Instead he'd called her the apple of his eye, and she'd believed him. A fisherman by trade, her father had never had much money, but he'd known how to care for his family. Most important to him was to raise his daughter to love the God of Israel. Of next importance had been to find Zlata a good and caring husband. He had succeeded on both counts.

When Zlata left her girlhood home on her wedding day— eleven years ago this month—she'd seen tenderness in the eyes of her waiting bridegroom. The look had calmed the fear of the sixteen-year-old girl she'd been. Her nerves had been chased away by his handsome smile. When Yerik promised to care for her always, she'd believed him. She'd learned to love him in the time they had together. Time that had been all too brief. Less than three years.

In those same three years, death swallowed her mother, her father, and her husband. And then, it had come for—

She squeezed her eyes shut, pushing away the memories and stopping the final one from taking their place.

This was her life. Living in the home of her in-laws, caring for their needs. Without the inheritance of her bride price from her father—money he'd spent in his desperate attempt to save her mother's life—Zlata had been left with nothing. Taneli and Abra could have cast her out. She might have starved to death long before this or been forced into an unspeakable way of life in order to survive. The thought terrified her, as so many things did. She should be grateful that she had not fallen into such circumstances. She *was* grateful. Yet she couldn't pretend it wasn't hard. Loneliness overwhelmed her at times. She felt invisible, afraid, forgotten, and her heart had been hardened by bitterness.

Dara's fingertips touched Zlata's shoulder. "The mistress sleeps."

Zlata looked and saw that it was true. Usually Abra's bad spells lasted much longer. Relieved for the change, she stood. "Then we should sleep too."

Dara nodded.

"I will see you in the morning."

Zlata didn't wait for confirmation from the young servant, nor did she take the candle the girl offered. She knew the placement of each room and the location of every piece of furniture in them. She could make her way through the house without trouble, even on the darkest of nights. Still, when she stepped out of the bedchamber, she was afraid she might stumble into her father-in-law in the dark. But she didn't, and soon enough she was lying on the mat in her own small room.

Sleep refused to come again. Instead her thoughts whirled backward in time, back to those few precious years with Yerik, back to when she'd discovered a new life was blossoming within her. For a time—for such a brief time—this had been a house filled with rejoicing. She'd known the love of her husband. She'd known the approval of her mother-in-law. Even Taneli had smiled upon her, for she was doing what God had intended her to do. She'd seen the years stretching before her in contented bliss. Yerik tending the family vineyards. Taneli teaching in the synagogue. Zlata, with the help of Abra, raising Yerik's children as they came along. Her heart had been full. Even the deaths of her parents hadn't completely marred her joy.

Bitterness rose like bile. How could God have allowed everything to go so wrong? Why had He taken her mother, her father, her husband, and finally her infant son? What sin had she committed to deserve such punishment?

Rolling onto her side, she allowed tears to wet her pillow. Weeping changed nothing, of course. In the morning she would still rise alone, as always. She would still be afraid. And the years that stretched before her would still be filled with sorrow.

The following day, Taneli's raised voice reached Zlata in the courtyard. Her father-in-law and his close friend, Nathan the Younger, had been debating points of the law for much of the morning, but now they had turned their attention upon a man called Yeshua the Nazarene. Zlata had heard of the teacher. Who in Capernaum didn't know his name? He was often mentioned by other women in the marketplace and at the well. Many miracles were attributed to him. It was rumored that

Yeshua had cured a demoniac the previous year. She remembered her father-in-law's reaction when he'd heard that this so-called healing had happened on the Sabbath.

Taneli was a righteous and learned man, a Pharisee, a man in authority at the synagogue in Capernaum. He was outraged that Yeshua, who had begun attracting larger crowds in recent months, would perform any kind of work on the Sabbath. A sure sign that he was not a prophet, as some had declared him to be. Yeshua was a charlatan, a nobody. Taneli didn't understand why the rabbi from Nazareth was allowed to teach in the synagogues throughout Galilee. Her father-in-law, try as he might, hadn't been able to stop it in Capernaum either.

Hearing the increasing rage in her father-in-law's voice, Zlata decided to make herself scarce lest he vent some of that anger in her direction. She hurried to gather the clothes for washing then left through the courtyard doorway.

The house of Taneli had many rooms that surrounded a fine courtyard. Its size proclaimed the success of the family vineyards to anyone who passed by. Built on a hillside, it had a fine view of the Sea of Galilee, especially from the rooftop. Oh, how Yerik had loved to stand on that rooftop and look out over the lake. He'd loved the water when the sky was clear and sunlight danced upon the glassy surface like a thousand stars. He'd loved it when storms blew through, the skies gray and the lake churning. Although her husband's work had been tied to the vineyards, his heart had leaned toward the Sea of Galilee.

Dear, sweet Yerik. She hadn't liked the idea of marriage when she was fifteen and first learned of the betrothal her father had arranged. Yerik had been a stranger to her. But in time, he'd won her heart with his kindness and with his laughter. His simple joy, his love of life, had infected everyone around him. Even Taneli had been different when with his son.

Zlata hardened her heart against the sweet memories. Better to beat back the rising emotions while she laundered the clothes. Better to let her tears mix with the wash water and soak into the earth, unseen. Like Zlata herself.

CHAPTER TWO

The improvement in Abra's health happened suddenly. One morning, when Zlata entered her mother-in-law's bedchamber, she found her sitting up in bed. Although still weak, her body was free of fever.

"Zlata, at last you have come. I am hungry."

"I will bring food at once." She turned to leave.

"Something sweet. A pear compote, I think."

She faced her mother-in-law again. "We have no dried pears, my lady."

"Then go buy some." Abra slid down on the pillows, her eyes drifting closed. "I will have bread to hold me until you return from the marketplace."

Zlata nodded then hurried from the room.

A short while later, she left the house. It was doubtful she would find what her mother-in-law had requested. Dried pears were not in abundance at this season of the year. But hopefully she would find something else to tempt Abra. Perhaps some berries or nuts.

Zlata hurried toward the marketplace, a breeze tugging at her headscarf. Of all the household duties that fell to her, this was her favorite. It allowed her to be away from the house, out from under scrutiny and criticism. It allowed her to listen to the gossip of other women and to hear news of the country that Taneli thought her too ignorant to understand. Going to the well provided those same opportunities, but that chore also meant carrying a heavy water jar back to the house. Her basket was normally much lighter when she returned from the market.

She wasn't far past the gate when she heard a woman say, "Judah can walk again. I saw him. He went to see Yeshua when he was teaching, and he came back walking."

"You are mistaken, Sarah. Judah will never walk again."

"I tell you, I am not mistaken. I saw it myself."

A third woman chimed in. "The teacher will be outside the city today. We could go and see him for ourselves."

"Judah is out there?"

"Not Judah. Yeshua. He is there with his disciples. People are going to see him, to see what he does. We should go too."

As Zlata listened to the women, her gaze took in the activity of the marketplace as well as the produce, fish, and grain available and the fabric for sale.

"I have no time for such nonsense," one of the women stated firmly.

Zlata had no time for it either. She should find what she came to buy and return to the house. Abra was waiting. But she would like to see this Nazarene for herself. She would like to see the teacher whose actions and words caused Taneli to rage against him. Two of the gossiping women set off through the gate. Zlata waited a few moments. Should she follow them? Taneli wouldn't approve, but he wouldn't know. And Abra was likely back to sleep again.

Her decision made, she hurried through the gate and away from town. She soon discovered she was one of many who wanted to see the teacher. Streams of people were on the road, all headed in the same direction. Soon they were climbing higher up a hillside. While others around her carried on conversations, Zlata began to worry about her mother-in-law waiting for her pear compote. Perhaps she should turn back. The marketplace must be empty by now since it seemed half of Capernaum was climbing this hillside with her.

And then she saw the even larger crowd up ahead, some seated on the ground, some standing in small clusters. A little higher above them, a man was addressing those around him, his arms outstretched. As others noticed him, they fell silent.

So that was the Nazarene. There was nothing especially remarkable about him, as far as she could tell. He wore an ordinary-colored tunic. Simple attire, befitting a carpenter or a fisherman or a weaver or even a shepherd. His hair was short, his beard rough. More evidence that he wasn't a man of means. He looked no different than most of the men surrounding him or the ones gathering to hear him speak.

Zlata weaved her way through the crowd, not ready to stop, wanting to be closer so she could hear him for herself. She *needed* to be closer for a reason beyond hearing, although she didn't understand why. Finally, when she could not go easily forward, she sank to the ground, looking up at the man she'd come to see.

As if he'd waited for her, Yeshua also sat, then began to speak again. "Blessed are the poor in spirit, for theirs is the kingdom of heaven." His voice rang clear and strong, carrying far beyond his closest followers, carrying far beyond Zlata. "Blessed are those who mourn, for they shall be comforted."

Blessed? She had mourned. She *still* mourned. But God had not blessed her. She'd gone without comfort for years. She lived in a frightening world with nothing of her own, with no one who cared for her. Certainly, there was no love lost between her and her in-laws. And after eight years alone, she understood that Taneli had no intention of finding her another husband. It suited him that she would die alone.

Blessed?

Bitter tears welled. She wished she hadn't come. She wished she'd done her shopping and returned to the house. She wished she could go back in time and choose a different path. She wished her life had turned out the way she'd once dreamed.

She'd hoped that in coming here… Oh, she didn't know what she'd hoped.

"You are the salt of the earth; but if the salt has become tasteless, how can it be made salty again? It is no longer good for anything, except to be thrown out and trampled underfoot by men."

I'm tasteless. I'm no longer good for anything. My womb will never carry another child. I will never be wanted by a husband. I've been thrown out. I've been trampled underfoot.

She remembered the look in Taneli's eyes after her son died in her arms. As if he believed she'd made her baby boy sick, the same way he blamed her for Yerik's death by a Roman sword. Sometimes she blamed herself for that. Yerik had meant to protect her, never guessing how the soldier would react. One moment he'd been alive, vibrant, joyful. The next, his life's blood had drained into the earth.

"But I say to you, do not resist an evil person; but whoever slaps you on your right cheek, turn the other to him also. If anyone wants to sue you and take your shirt, let him have your coat also. Whoever forces you to go one mile, go with him two."

Zlata thought of everything that had been taken from her. Her parents. Her husband. Her child. Her home. Her losses were more than a slap on the cheek or a cloak off her back or the journey of a mile. She'd lost everything. She had nothing more to give. Nothing.

"But I say to you, love your enemies and pray for those who persecute you."

Love the Romans? Pray for Taneli? Impossible!

Eyes downcast, she pushed to her feet and hurried down the slope, almost tripping over people in her rush to escape, tears streaking her cheeks.

Her father-in-law was right. Yeshua the Nazarene was a madman.

On the following afternoon, Zlata sat in a shady corner, mending in her lap. On the opposite side of the courtyard, Taneli and Simon, another Pharisee, conversed, having returned from the synagogue not long before. Matching frowns creased their foreheads.

Stroking his beard, Taneli said, "The people are always running after one teacher or another. They are fools. Sheep. It is the same with this Yeshua. It won't last. It cannot last."

"It has lasted too long already," Simon responded. "Why aren't they outraged when he consorts with sinners? And not sinners alone. Enemies of Israel as well."

"Bah."

Simon leaned forward. "After the centurion's servant got up from his sickbed, Yeshua said the Roman had greater faith than anyone in Israel."

Taneli growled something unintelligible as he looked across the courtyard.

Zlata hastily lowered her gaze to the tunic, lest her father-in-law discover her watching and listening. Most of the time, he paid no heed to her at all. Better that it stay that way.

Before long, the two men resumed talking, but their voices were lower now, making it hard to understand their words. No matter. She didn't want to hear anything more about the Nazarene. Her one encounter with him had disappointed her. But what had she expected? She no longer believed in miracles, if she ever had.

Expelling a quick breath, she gathered the mending, stood, and went inside. When she entered the bedchamber, her mother-in-law was sitting up in bed. Abra's sister, Hadassah, sat on a stool beside the bed. Zlata nodded in their direction before putting away the clothing she carried.

"It's true," Hadassah said in an excited voice. "The centurion's servant was healed at the moment Yeshua said it was so. He was up and waiting on the household by the time the officer returned home."

"I do not believe it."

"Everyone in town is talking about it."

"It's a story made up by the man's disciples. They pay people to pass these rumors on. Taneli knows. They depend upon people like you to spread their stories. His followers are all liars. Charlatans."

"Perhaps he would have healed you if Taneli had asked him."

Abra sucked in a breath. "Don't let my husband hear you say such a thing."

Zlata didn't want to hear it either. With another nod toward her mother-in-law, she left the bedchamber. Feeling restless, she climbed to the roof where she could stand and look out over the sea. But talk of the centurion and his servant stayed in her thoughts.

How could a Jew say anything respectful about a Roman? They were thugs. They were murderers. They were idolaters. To label one of them a man of great faith was wrong. So very wrong.

In her mind, she saw another beautiful spring day when she had walked with Yerik along the road to Magdala. How handsome her husband had looked, his beard freshly trimmed, his dark eyes alight with happiness. He'd worn a new tunic, one that she'd made him for his birthday. She remembered his smile as he'd shared that morning's good news. He'd been trying to buy a particular parcel of land for several months and had just received word that his latest offer had been accepted.

"An inheritance for Uriah," he'd said, speaking of their infant son.

The soldiers seemed to come out of nowhere, filling the road, moving fast. Zlata had been slow to react. A Roman had given her a shove, knocking her to the ground. Yerik moved to help her, to protect her from the heavy feet pounding the earth. He had held no malice in his movement, only a need to shelter his wife. Yet suddenly a sword had been unsheathed. Zlata hadn't seen the weapon enter her husband's abdomen, but she had seen the blood that flowed from the wound, staining his new tunic. She had screamed as he crumpled to the earth. She had gathered him in her arms and wept as she watched the light of life drain from his beautiful eyes.

Zlata blinked away the memories along with a rush of tears. Eight years had passed since that dreadful day. Shouldn't her sorrow have passed as well? Would there ever be a time when her heart didn't feel Yerik's absence and the cause of it? Would there be a time when the sight of a Roman soldier didn't bring terror with it?

Her gaze went to the sea. Not for the first time, she wished that the soldier had killed her that day as well.

CHAPTER THREE

Funnels of dust whirled on the road ahead of Zlata as she hurried on her errand. She carried a message from Taneli to Joel, the steward of his vineyards. Joel had been a worker under Yerik for several years before her husband's death. Afterward, he'd been promoted to steward. Perhaps that was why Zlata disliked him—because her loss had been his gain. No matter the reason, she always hated it when she was sent to the vineyard, and she particularly disliked talking to Joel.

Directed by other workers, she found the steward on a hillside, inspecting the vines. She stopped some distance away, silent, waiting.

When he turned and saw her, he smiled. He wasn't tall or good looking, as Yerik had been. He was ordinary in almost every way. He'd come to work in Capernaum when he'd been no more than sixteen, sent north after the death of his father. Local gossip said he had no other family. A friend had gained him employment with Yerik.

"Good day, Zlata," he greeted her.

"Joel." She nodded as she lowered her eyes, mindful that in most circumstances it was prohibited for a woman to talk with a man who wasn't a member of her family. Which made her wonder why Taneli sent her on these errands. Perhaps he did it to test her or to shame her in some way. She couldn't be sure.

"What brings you to the vineyard on this hot day?" Joel asked, wiping the sweat from his brow.

"I have a message from the master." She relayed Taneli's words exactly as he'd given them to her.

"Tell Taneli it will be done," he responded. "Just as he wants."

She nodded and turned away.

"Zlata."

She tried to ignore him but couldn't. She was ignored so often herself. How could she do the same to another? She faced him again. "Yes?"

"Will I see you at the wedding feast next week?"

"Wedding feast?" she echoed, as if she didn't know what he meant.

"Yitzhak and Zillah's."

"No. I will not be there. My mother-in-law has need of me."

"I heard her health is much improved."

Zlata shook her head. "Abra is better, but I will not leave her."

How could she explain to someone like Joel why she didn't want to go? Weddings were joyous events. The celebration often went on for days. Zlata used to love going to them with her parents and, later, with her husband. As a young woman, she'd often been counted among a bride's companions. She assisted the bride as she donned her beautiful bridal attire, helping her to look like a queen. Then, along with all the other companions, Zlata was sent out to meet the groom, also resplendent in his wedding garments. Zlata had laughed and rejoiced with the others. She had taken part in everything. She had danced. She had eaten the food and drunk the wine. Oh, the joy of those celebrations.

But she no longer wished to see the happiness of a bride and groom as they began their new life together. Her own marriage had ended in tragedy, and all she had to offer others was her sorrow.

"You will be missed," Joel said, drawing her attention back to him. His eyes were filled with compassion.

The unexpected look caused her breath to catch. "I must go." She turned and started down the hillside. This time Joel didn't call after her. This time she didn't look back.

On her return from the vineyard, Zlata stopped outside the home she'd once shared with Yerik. Her husband had often told her that he started building it the day after he first saw her walking to the well, a large jug balanced on her shoulder. He said he knew in that moment he wanted her to be his bride. While Taneli would have hired workmen to build his son a fine home, Yerik had wanted to do it with his own hands, proof of the commitment he was ready to make. Six months later, the betrothal had been struck. Less than a year after that, the two had married.

Unlike her husband, Zlata hadn't been raised in wealth and privilege. Her father had been a fisherman, like so many other men in this town located at the northern end of the Sea of Galilee. The family's home had been a simple one. A single room on the street level, plus an upper room reached by stairs on the side of the house. Very much like the house Zlata had moved into on her wedding day.

She'd been happy here. So very happy.

Drawing a breath, she turned and lifted her eyes toward the spacious house of her in-laws. Taneli employed a number of servants who took care of the cleaning and cooking as well as tending to the animals. Zlata helped wherever she was needed, but she wasn't paid for her work as the servants were. She was, after all, family, and expected to do Taneli's and Abra's bidding.

Family?

Resentment left a bad taste in her mouth.

"Trust the Lord," her mother's voice whispered in her memory. *"Trust Him always."*

She closed her eyes. "O Lord, our Lord, how majestic is Your name in all the earth."

When she was younger, she'd whispered those words with such faith. She'd wanted nothing more than to declare the glory of God. But her faith had shriveled over time. It was more difficult to trust now than it once had been.

More difficult? Almost impossible.

"O Lord, our Lord, how majestic is Your name in all the earth."

A memory of Yeshua on the hillside standing, then sitting, popped into her mind. She remembered the authority in his voice as he'd spoken. Such strength in his words and yet such gentleness too. There had been something…something about him.

She gave her head a shake. If she'd needed proof of how weak her faith had become, thinking about the Nazarene while trying to praise God should do it.

I'm lost and alone. I'm tired. My heart has withered within me.

And so would it be until the day she died. Nothing could change her life for the better now.

CHAPTER FOUR

Zlata walked swiftly on the road away from town, a basket slung over one arm. It was preparation day, and all of the servants in Taneli's household were making ready for the beginning of the Sabbath. Meats were roasting over the fire. A savory stew was simmering in a pot. Loaves of bread had been baked. Fruits and vegetables were ready to serve.

One thing alone was missing. Flowers. Abra liked to decorate the house with fresh flowers for the Sabbath. She said they were a feast for the eyes and a way to honor God with their beauty. On this matter, Zlata agreed with her mother-in-law.

It was early enough in the season for the wildflowers to be blooming in abundance. It wasn't difficult to find a field that was alive with them. Zlata left the road and began to pick them, placing them carefully in the basket. There was a profusion of color. Yellow and pink, blue and lavender, red and white.

For a moment, she felt a spark of happiness. She felt young again, with a life full of promise ahead of her. She was tempted to lie down in the long grass amid the wildflowers, to stare up at the sky, to name all of the different shapes the clouds made as they drifted overhead.

But a sound from the road drew her gaze, and she saw soldiers hurrying along it toward town. Sucking in a breath, she stepped into the shade of a nearby tree, hoping she hadn't been seen. All too familiar fear tightened her throat as she watched them go. She didn't breathe another easy breath until they turned a bend in the road and disappeared from view.

She had almost relaxed enough to return to her flower picking when a sound of rustling grass caused her to jump, afraid that she might have disturbed a snake or some other creature. Then, between two trees, a large, motley-looking dog bounded into view, its tongue lolling out of one side of its mouth. It ran straight for her, not stopping until it lifted its front paws and smacked her in the chest, knocking her down. Her fear might have returned if its next act hadn't been to slap her in the face with its tongue.

"Stop!" Eyes closed, she protected her mouth with her hands. "Go away."

"Reuben! Get off of her."

The man's voice caused Zlata to bolt upright. The dog backed away at the same time.

"I'm sorry." The man stood in the shadows of another tree. "Reuben isn't very obedient."

"No. He isn't." She got quickly to her feet, her hands checking to make certain her headscarf was in place.

"He isn't mean. Only enthusiastic." He stepped into the sunlight.

She recognized him then and a small gasp escaped her. It was Alphaeus's son, Levi, a despised tax collector in Capernaum. Only, Levi didn't look the way she remembered him. He'd been a man who hid from his fellow Jews when not seated in the tax booth. A man who was furtive, on edge, his eyes darting this way and that.

"Reuben, come." He motioned for the dog to join him. When it did, it looked up at its master with what could only be called an adoring, trusting gaze.

Zlata picked up her basket. She didn't have nearly enough flowers yet.

"You're Zlata, the widow of Yerik, aren't you?"

Her breath caught again. It wasn't good to be singled out by such a man.

"You needn't worry. I'm not a tax collector any longer."

She drew back. "You aren't?" Her eyes widened in surprise. How had she not heard about that? Surely it had been gossiped about in the marketplace and throughout Capernaum.

He gave his head a slow shake. "No, the master called me in the autumn, and I got up and followed him."

"The master?"

"Yeshua." As he spoke the name, he smiled. It altered his appearance even more than before.

"The Nazarene," she whispered.

"Yes."

She should have forgotten gathering more flowers. She should have turned on her heel and walked away without another word, without another thought. Instead, she asked, "Why did you follow him?"

"Because he has the answers. Because he is the one all Israel has long awaited. Because he teaches the Law and the Prophets and the Writings as no one else I have ever heard.

Even when I don't fully understand what he teaches, I understand more than I did before." Enthusiasm filled Levi's voice, increasing with each new word.

She shook her head. "I went to hear Yeshua not long ago. I could not believe what he teaches is right."

Sympathy filled Levi's eyes. "Then you didn't listen long enough, widow of Yerik."

Words rang in her memory: "*Blessed are those who mourn…. You are the salt of the earth…. Whoever slaps you on your right cheek, turn the other to him also…. Love your enemies and pray for those who persecute you….*"

"I listened," she said, anger twisting in her belly.

Levi patted the dog's head as he looked at Zlata in silence. After what seemed a long while, he offered another smile. "When you are able, listen again. Perhaps you will hear with new ears." He glanced down. "Come, Reuben. We must go."

With that, the former tax collector and his dog strode away, disappearing once again between the trees.

Listen again…. Hear with new ears. Everyone seemed to be talking nonsense these days.

Zlata returned to the task of gathering flowers.

CHAPTER FIVE

On the first day of the week, Zlata knelt in the garden, tending to the vegetables growing there. The scent of a savory stew wafted to her from across the courtyard and made her stomach growl in anticipation. But she had a lengthy wait before it would be time to eat. When her gardening was done, she was to go into town for some fabric. Abra, now that she was feeling so much better, wanted a new tunic made. An elegant new tunic.

The courtyard door opened, and Taneli and Nathan the younger entered. Both of them wore grim expressions, but there was thunder in her father-in-law's eyes.

What now?

"We must expose him," Taneli said, his voice carrying across the courtyard. "There are too many who hang on his every word. We must make them see he doesn't speak the truth."

Ah. The teacher again. Taneli's temper grew worse by the day because of Yeshua the Nazarene. Her father-in-law's determination to see the teacher discredited had become an obsession. As far as Zlata could tell, it was in the forefront of his mind when he arose in the morning and when he retired for the night.

"We'll have a chance tomorrow," Nathan responded. "There will be many at Simon's house for supper. We'll trap him in a falsehood. We'll trick him into admitting he has lied. We will find a way to make others see that he breaks the law at every turn."

"If my wife hadn't been unwell all these weeks, I would have thought to have a dinner myself. I could have brought leaders from Jerusalem perhaps. They would have discovered a way to stop him long before now."

"You've had much to concern you, my friend. It is enough that you will be present at the dinner. You search the scriptures. You will know what to say and when to say it."

Taneli grunted. Then he smiled, an expression devoid of humor.

A shiver ran up Zlata's spine. Fear tightened her chest. Fear for someone other than herself. Which made no sense. Yeshua was nothing to her. The little she'd heard him say on that hillside had been enough to convince her he was not who some thought him to be. He was not a learned man, like Taneli. He was a carpenter. He couldn't be a prophet. A prophet would condemn the Romans and never speak of loving one's enemies. Above all else, Yeshua couldn't be the Messiah, as some suggested. He was nothing. He was nobody.

"They say," Nathan continued as the two men settled onto benches in the shade, "that he declared John the Baptist greater than anyone born of woman. And he says those of us who refuse to be baptized have rejected God's message."

"Outrageous!"

Zlata had heard others talk about John the Baptist. A wild man who demanded people confess their sins, and when they did, he baptized them in the river. A baptism of repentance.

"The Baptist called us vipers," Taneli said, almost spitting the words. "He threatened that we would be winnowed out. How can you call such a man great? He's a lunatic."

Nathan waved a hand in front of his face. "He is nothing. He'll soon be forgotten."

Taneli was undoubtedly right about John the Baptist. The same would be true of Yeshua the Nazarene. Both would soon be forgotten.

She pushed herself up from the ground then made her way inside. It was time she was on her way to the marketplace.

It didn't take Zlata long to find the right fabric for Abra's new tunic. She knew her mother-in-law's taste in colors and patterns well. Abra had declared Zlata an expert with needle and thread long before Yerik's death and had often asked her daughter-in-law to make her new garments.

"You have the most nimble fingers," she had said.

Abra no longer asked Zlata to sew for her. It was expected, demanded, like every other duty that fell to her.

"Greetings, Zlata."

She turned from a booth to see Channah, a servant in the home of Simon the Pharisee. Channah was about sixteen and had a sadness in her dark eyes that drew Zlata to her in empathy. Simon had brought the girl to Capernaum from Jerusalem a couple of years ago, and her extreme shyness had kept her an outsider.

"Hello, Channah."

"My master says you will help me serve at the dinner tomorrow."

Zlata shook her head, not understanding.

"You weren't told?" Channah's gaze dropped, and she seemed to shrink into herself. "Oh. Then you won't be coming."

Tomorrow. At Simon's house. She remembered Taneli and Nathan's discussion. This must have been what they meant. A dinner…where they planned to trap Yeshua in some way.

Simon's servant turned away without another word.

"Channah?"

The girl looked back.

"I haven't been told it is so, but I believe I am to be there. I heard Taneli speak of the dinner earlier today."

A shy smile tweaked the corners of Channah's mouth.

Zlata returned the smile. Then they went their separate ways.

In no hurry to return home, Zlata perused items in other stalls and booths. As usual, the marketplace was filled with sounds—sellers shouting encouragement to buy their wares, sheep and goats bleating, birds calling, people talking. The smell of spices, cooking food, and animals filled the air. She spoke to a few other women, but she wasn't tempted to linger in conversation. Too often they spoke of their husbands or their children, and those topics remained painful to Zlata, a reminder of what she had lost and would never have again.

"It *was* Bilhah. I saw her with my own eyes."

The words were spoken in a loud whisper. Loud enough for Zlata to hear. But it was the name that caused her to stop and listen.

"I thought she left Capernaum."

Zlata turned to see the women who gossiped nearby, their heads close together, foreheads almost touching.

"No. She was there on the hillside, listening to Yeshua. She stood against a tree. I don't think she wanted to be seen. Afraid, no doubt, of how others would treat her. Or afraid Yeshua would tell her to be gone. But there she stood. She was trans-fixed by the rabbi. She didn't even notice me."

"Shameful." The woman *tsked, tsked*. "Shameful."

Zlata's stomach clenched. She hadn't seen Bilhah for many years, but she'd heard what had happened to her girlhood friend. Bilhah had been widowed the year before the same hap-pened to Zlata. Her husband had drowned in a fishing accident. Similar to Zlata, Bilhah had no parents, no siblings, no extended family to turn to. Unlike Zlata, Bilhah's in-laws lived far away and had offered no help to the beautiful widow. Without a source of income or family to help her, desperation had driven Bilhah to survive in the only way she could. A way of shame.

A shudder ran through Zlata as she moved away from the gossiping women.

It could easily have been her others whispered about in the marketplace, if not for a place with her in-laws. She had nothing of her own beyond her clothing and two small coins that Yerik had given her on the morning of the day he died. She would never spend those coins. Not now. Not ever. Not even if she was in Bilhah's position. Those coins represented a link to the past, to a much happier time. So she kept them tucked away, a secret treasure, wrapped in a blue scarf.

Once beyond the crowded market, she quickened her footsteps. She didn't want to see or speak to anyone else today. Remembering her friend had made her sad while reminding her how tenuous her life was.

I could be Bilhah, living on the edges, barely surviving, having to sell myself.

The thought sickened her and caused fear to shiver up her spine.

Bilhah. Men had always noticed her, and women had always liked her. Her eyes had been dark pools. Her deep umber hair lush and shiny. When she smiled, others had felt happy, carefree. When she married, it had been for love. Her husband, a fisherman like so many in Capernaum, had doted on her. Their lives had been simple but full of joy. Bilhah had been gloriously happy, even in her poverty. For a time.

Oh, Bilhah. I'm sorry. I should have tried to help you while I could.

When she reached Taneli's house, she opened the door to the courtyard and was surprised to see her mother-in-law seated in the shade.

"Finally," Abra said, motioning for Zlata to come closer. "I thought you would never get back. Did you find what I wanted?"

"I believe you will like this, my lady." She placed the fabric in her mother-in-law's lap.

"Yes, this will do nicely. You'll have it ready before the wedding." She sighed heavily. "I don't want to make do with one of my old ones."

Zlata bit the inside of her lip. She wanted to say most women in Capernaum had only one tunic, perhaps two if they were very blessed. But of course she couldn't say such a thing. It wasn't her place.

Abra flicked her wrist, a gesture of dismissal, a wordless command for Zlata to be about her duties. She left in silence.

CHAPTER SIX

A warm breeze moved through Capernaum the next day as Zlata swept Simon's house in preparation for the dinner. In the courtyard, two of the Pharisee's servants were preparing food for the expected guests while their master and Zlata's father-in-law visited in the shade. Abra had disappeared to another room in the house. Perhaps she and their hostess had retreated to a place on the roof to catch more of the lake breeze.

Simon's home was modest compared to Taneli's, but there was still significant space. Zlata wondered how many had been invited to recline at table with the Pharisee. Would Yeshua come alone, or would some of his disciples be with him? Were other Pharisees and scribes expected? Did Yeshua know the invitation was a trap, that they wanted to discredit him…or something worse?

She didn't understand why it mattered to her. She wasn't one of Yeshua's followers. She didn't believe him to be a prophet. She didn't think he was a gifted or profound teacher. And yet she didn't want harm to come to him.

Harm? What harm could her father-in-law or the other Pharisees and scribes do to him? Being discredited did no actual harm. Did it? But if he broke the law, perhaps they could have him arrested. Did they have real cause to do that to him? She wasn't sure.

She paused in her sweeping to look out the doorway. Taneli looked grim, as always. Simon, on the other hand, appeared eager, excited. She imagined him rubbing his hands together in anticipation of a delicious delicacy.

El Shaddai, protect Yeshua.

The silent plea came from a deep place within Zlata. It was all the more surprising because she hadn't prayed in such a long time. Not spontaneous prayers. Not heartfelt ones. And never for a stranger.

"Zlata, can you help me with these?"

She turned toward Channah. The younger servant had begun to arrange cushions on the couches that surrounded three sides of the large table.

"Yes." She put aside the broom then went to the opposite side of the table to arrange cushions there.

As was tradition, the head of the table had enough room for three people, including the host and his guest of honor. Several more could recline comfortably on the left and several on the right. Their placements would be by order of age or importance. Spectators would be allowed into the courtyard where they could view the festivities and, perhaps, partake of leftover food when the meal was done. Crumbs from the table for the poor.

Sounds from the courtyard drew both Channah and Zlata to the wide doorway. They watched as Yeshua spoke to Simon. His smile was warm, and he seemed completely at ease. Unlike

Zlata, who felt the tension knotting her belly. Behind Yeshua were three men she recognized from the previous week when she'd gone with the crowd to hear the teacher speak. They had been close to him that day as well. Some of his disciples, no doubt. She was glad they were with the rabbi. This way he wouldn't be outnumbered by those who wanted to be rid of him.

Yeshua and his men moved deeper into the courtyard, allowing Simon to greet three more guests. Nathan the younger was one of them.

Zlata felt the knot in her stomach harden. Simon hadn't kissed Yeshua in greeting. He hadn't offered water to wash his feet. A man like Simon didn't forget such courtesies. His rudeness must be intentional, she thought, and Taneli's smile confirmed her suspicions.

Yeshua stopped and spoke to the female servants by the cooking fire. His voice was gentle, his words kind. His attention seemed to please the young women.

Then Yeshua's gaze lifted to the doorway, and he looked straight at Zlata. It made her breath catch in her chest. She took a quick step backward, into the shadows of the room. She turned away, not wanting to see what else transpired. She wished she could go home. She wished she hadn't been told to help serve the tables. She didn't want to be a witness to whatever Simon and her father-in-law had planned.

"Come, everyone." The host's voice carried to her. "Let us eat."

She scurried into a corner, like a mouse hiding from a cat.

Simon led the way into the house, ushering Yeshua to the place of honor. Taneli and Simon flanked him at the head of the table. The others reclined on the couches in their respective spots.

"Zlata," Channah whispered, "it's time to serve."

Ducking her head, Zlata followed the girl outside. A short while later, she returned with a large platter of roasted meat. Channah followed with a tray of vegetables. Bread, butter, and wine were added as quickly as possible.

The men around the table talked of many things as they ate. Several different conversations went on at once, creating a kind of deep buzzing sound in the room. When not serving, Zlata stood against the wall, watching for the moment when someone might motion for something. Mostly her gaze remained on Yeshua. He seemed oblivious to the animosity of Simon and Taneli and their friends. He spoke to the men with confidence, and he smiled frequently.

When would they trap him? What were they planning?

She looked toward the disciples who had come with Yeshua. They were seated at the end of the table, two on one side, one on the other. Were they as unaware of the danger as their teacher?

Beyond the wide doorway to the courtyard, people had begun to gather. Many of them had settled onto the ground and held their own conversations.

Looking at them, Zlata was reminded of another banquet when she had been just a girl. A well-known rabbi had come to Capernaum. Her parents had sat in a courtyard much like the one outside this house, hoping to hear him teach through the open doorways. Zlata had been too young to care what the man had to say. She'd cared more about the dog in the far corner of the courtyard. She'd sat on the ground beside it, stroking its golden-brown coat and rubbing its ears. She'd wished she had a dog like that one, to play with, to sleep with.

It was the collective gasp of the spectators toward the end of the meal that pulled Zlata back to the present and her gaze back to Yeshua. Behind where he reclined stood a woman, her head down, hair and scarf hiding her face, her shoulders slumped, a posture of shame. Definitely not another household servant. The woman had come from the streets but hadn't remained in the courtyard.

Zlata was about to look toward Channah, wondering what should be done, when the woman lifted her head. She was weeping, but it didn't disguise her identity.

"Bilhah," Zlata whispered on a stunned breath.

As everyone watched, her girlhood friend knelt down on the floor, her tears continuing to fall, wetting Yeshua's feet where they rested at the edge of the couch. She used her own hair to wipe away the dampness. Then she kissed his feet—accompanied by another, louder collective gasp—before she opened a vial and poured perfume where her lips had touched. Afterward she kissed his feet again and again.

The room had gone completely silent. Zlata barely drew breath as she watched, waiting for some terrible reaction. She expected someone to grab Bilhah by the hair and drag her from the room. Or worse.

Instead, Yeshua turned his gaze upon his host. "Simon, I have something to say to you."

"Say it, Teacher."

"A moneylender had two debtors: one owed five hundred denarii, and the other fifty. When they were unable to repay, he graciously forgave them both. So which of them will love him more?"

That was easy, Zlata thought. The one who owed the most. The one who owed five hundred denarii.

Simon, far more learned than Zlata, confirmed her silent answer. "I suppose the one whom he forgave more."

"You have judged correctly," Yeshua answered with a slight nod. Then he turned on the couch to look at Bilhah, still kneeling near his feet. But when he spoke, his words continued to address Simon. "Do you see this woman? I entered your house; you gave Me no water for My feet, but she has wet My feet with her tears and wiped them with her hair."

Something tightened in Zlata's chest. She'd seen the insult with her own eyes.

"You gave Me no kiss; but she, since the time I came in, has not ceased to kiss My feet."

Zlata looked at Bilhah, her head dipped forward and her hair once against hiding her face.

"You did not anoint My head with oil, but she anointed My feet with perfume. For this reason I say to you, her sins, which are many, have been forgiven, for she loved much; but he who is forgiven little, loves little."

Yeshua paused, and perhaps it was the silence that caused Bilhah to stand and meet his gaze. The tenderest of looks filled his eyes. His voice softened. "Your sins have been forgiven."

Who is this man who even forgives sins?

Yeshua's gaze shifted from Bilhah to Zlata. Although she was far from an oil lamp and hidden in shadows, it seemed that Yeshua not only saw her face but that he could see into her heart as well. The look, still full of kindness, stole the breath from her lungs.

Then the teacher turned his eyes once more upon Bilhah. "Your faith has saved you; go in peace."

Bilhah's expression changed in an instant. It was far more than her natural beauty that could be seen by everyone present. It was more than the sweet smile that curved her mouth. It was a comeliness that radiated from within. And when she walked away from the table, it was with her head held high, her shoulders no longer slumped.

CHAPTER SEVEN

Daybreak was only a promise when Zlata opened her eyes after a short and restless night. She had lain awake for hours, replaying the dinner at Simon's over and over again. Mostly she'd thought about Bilhah, about the change in her expression when Yeshua said, *"Your faith has saved you; go in peace."*

He forgave her sins. How can he do that? Only Adonai can forgive sins. Only by following the laws of our fathers can we earn the Lord's mercy.

And yet it seemed Zlata had actually *seen* forgiveness flow from Yeshua and over Bilhah. Impossible but true.

She closed her eyes, remembering the moment Yeshua had lifted his gaze to her. He'd *seen* her, even standing in the shadows. A servant. A woman. A widow. He hadn't merely looked at her. He'd *seen* her. Had he seen the bitterness in her heart too? Had he understood the hatred she felt for the Romans? Had he known how empty and alone and neglected she felt? Had he understood the fear that daily dogged her heels? Was she in need of his forgiveness too?

Ridiculous. Who was Yeshua of Nazareth to forgive Bilhah her sins? How could Zlata even think she'd seen such forgiveness happen? She shoved aside the light covering on her bed, rose, and made ready for the day.

A short while later, she sat beside the small mill in the courtyard, grinding wheat. It took her more than an hour a day to grind enough flour for Taneli's household. Of course, her father-in-law could well afford to purchase flour already ground by Gershom the miller. Gershom used a donkey to turn the stone at the large hourglass-shaped grinder and was able to produce large quantities of flour every hour. But Taneli believed that an unnecessary expense. Perhaps he would think differently if the tedious work fell to him instead of an insignificant woman.

Insignificant.

Again, she recalled Yeshua's eyes as he'd looked at her. In that instant, she hadn't felt insignificant. There had been something so tender and understanding in his gaze. More than that. Something undefinable but beautiful.

Taneli hadn't felt that way, of course. He'd been infuriated by all that happened at the dinner. No matter what he or his friends tried, Yeshua hadn't seemed concerned. He'd conversed with the men as if they were on friendly terms.

Zlata smiled as she remembered Yeshua's audacity after Bilhah had anointed his feet, when he'd pointed out Simon's rudeness as a host. It was something Taneli hadn't stopped talking about after returning home. Zlata supposed it was a sin to take so much pleasure in her father-in-law's extreme frustration, but she couldn't help it. The memory of it seemed to lighten the task of grinding wheat.

Three days later, in the cool air of early morning, Zlata made her way to the well. A breeze tugged at her headscarf and the hem of her tunic. It made her think of happier times when she was a little girl. She had loved to walk beside her mother to fetch water for their household. Although Zlata's water jar had been small, suited to her own size, she'd delighted in balancing it on her shoulder, mimicking her mother who'd carried the much larger jar.

"You are good to help me, Zlata." Her mother's smile had felt like sunshine. "Soon you will do this all by yourself."

Oh, how grown-up that had made her feel. Sometimes, she'd walked around on tiptoe, hoping her mother would think her taller and that the time had arrived for that solo chore.

The sweet memories seemed to shorten the walk, and suddenly she heard other girls and women exchanging small talk as they waited to fill their water jars at the cistern.

Zlata no longer felt on equal footing with the young wives and mothers who had once been her friends and acquaintances. She owned nothing and had no one. She was a poor and childless widow. Her husband had been slain and her infant son had died. Surely it was a punishment from Adonai. The other women weren't unkind to her, but neither did she feel included in their midst. They were contented. She was… not. And so, an outsider by circumstance, she listened as they talked.

"He travels from village to village, teaching about the kingdom of God wherever he goes."

"Many of his disciples are from right here in Capernaum. Simon, the one he calls Cephas, is among them. They've all gone with him."

"Yes, and some women are with him too. Mary who is called Magdalene is one of them. They say he cast out sickness and evil spirits from her, and now she helps support his ministry from her own wealth. And Joanna, the wife of Chuza, is a supporter too."

Zlata didn't need to ask of whom they spoke. She wondered if the rabbi had left Capernaum and begun teaching elsewhere because of Taneli and other men like him. But when she remembered how Yeshua had looked, reclining at Simon's table, she was certain his comings and goings had nothing to do with the religious leaders of Galilee. He was not a man to feel threatened, even when it would be wise to do so.

"He is merciful and kind. And wise. I would like to hear him teach again."

"Don't let your head be turned," another woman scolded.

A space at the well opened at last, and Zlata filled her jar with water. After hefting it to her shoulder, she nodded toward the others and began the walk back to Taneli's house. She had rounded a bend in the road when she heard someone call her name. She stopped and looked behind her, expecting to see one of the women who'd been at the well. But the road was empty.

"Zlata."

Movement behind a nearby tree drew her gaze. A moment later she whispered, "Bilhah?"

Her friend stepped fully into view. "I wasn't sure you would speak to me."

"Of course I will speak to you."

A smile played across Bilhah's lips. "Thank you."

"I was there," Zlata added softly. "At the house of Simon."

"I know. I saw you serving at the table before I entered from the courtyard."

"You look…" She couldn't find the right word. Different? Serene? Peaceful? Radiant?

Forgiven.

"I am changed," Bilhah said, as if reading Zlata's thoughts. Her words were filled with both certainty and wonder.

Zlata nodded, her throat tight with unexpected emotion.

"My old way of life is behind me. I've been given work by Jonah the weaver. I have a place to sleep that is my own."

"Oh, Bilhah. I am glad for you."

"And you?" There was tender concern in her friend's voice. "Are you well?"

"I am…content." Feeling the lie on her tongue, Zlata lowered her gaze.

"When Yeshua returns to Capernaum, go to hear him teach."

"Taneli wouldn't approve."

"Go, Zlata. Hear him. Truly listen. Learn from him."

Her father-in-law thought it foolishness to teach a woman. A waste. Even a sin. Taneli would never think to speak to a woman outside of his own household, unless it was to correct some sinful behavior. Rarely did he say more than a single word to Zlata, and even that seemed to pain him. There was no warmth between him and his wife either. There was respect, perhaps, but no love. Not the way it had been between Zlata's mother and father. Not the way it had been between her and Yerik.

"Yeshua can show you the way," Bilhah added.

She looked up again. "The way?"

"He will show you what the kingdom of God is like. It is… so much more than we think. *He* is so much more than we think."

Zlata turned. "I must get back with the water. I will be missed."

"When Yeshua returns, find him, Zlata. Listen to him teach. You'll see that I'm right."

"Goodbye, Bilhah. I wish you well."

She hurried on her way.

CHAPTER EIGHT

In the morning, two days after Zlata had spoken with Bilhah, she walked to a secluded spot near the lakeshore and settled onto the ground. For a few moments, she allowed herself to take pleasure in the way the light danced upon the water's surface.

But it wasn't long before her thoughts returned to that brief encounter with her old friend. The change in Bilhah had been even more remarkable then than on the night Yeshua told her she was forgiven. Such peace. It had surrounded her in an almost tangible way.

"Go, Zlata. Hear him. Truly listen. Learn from him."

She'd seen him. She'd tried listening to him. He hadn't said anything she cared to hear again.

"He will show you what the kingdom of God is like. It is…so much more than we think. He is so much more than we think."

Zlata remembered the look of compassion in the rabbi's eyes. Compassion but even more than that. So different from anything she had experienced in her lifetime.

"When Yeshua returns, find him, Zlata. Listen to him teach. You'll see that I'm right."

She shook her head, as if trying to drive away the memory. Why did her thoughts continue to turn to the Nazarene? Time and again. Was it only because everyone else seemed to talk about him so much? Taneli and his friends. Abra and her sister. Women at the well. Men in the marketplace. And now Bilhah.

Footsteps drew her eyes once again toward the lake. A man was following the waterline. As he drew closer, she recognized him. It was Zebedee, a man of some position in Capernaum who owned two fishing boats. He and his wife, Salome, had been friends with her parents.

Before she could wonder if Zebedee would recognize her too, he smiled and called her name. "Zlata." He stopped walking.

She rose from the ground. "Greetings, Zebedee."

"You are well?" He approached her.

"I am well. And you?"

"Well."

"And Salome?"

"She is in good health, God be praised." His gaze went to the lake. "The fishing was not the best the past few days. But that will change. It always does. I will spend today mending nets. With my sons away…" His words drifted into silence.

"Your sons have left Capernaum?" She remembered James and John. Hard workers like their father and hers.

"They follow Yeshua."

Zlata frowned. "They have left you to do the fishing on your own?" What sort of sons did that? Zebedee was no longer a young man. What if he couldn't keep up with the work? True, he wasn't without means. He could hire other fishermen. But was that any reason for James and John to abandon their duty to their own father?

"I was glad for them to go." Zebedee looked at Zlata again, his expression altering.

She suspected he'd had this same discussion with others. Perhaps many others.

"They are learning more than I could ever hope to teach them. They have a new master now, and their place is with him."

It wasn't unknown in Israel for young men to sometimes uproot their lives in order to follow a particular rabbi, to seek to understand the books of the Torah, to grow in their knowledge of God. Still, it seemed strange to Zlata for James and John to have done so. The young men she remembered hadn't seemed the sort.

"Do you have time to sit and talk?" Zebedee asked, motioning toward a raised bank.

She nodded, and they made their way to it.

Once settled, Zebedee began. "I admit, I wasn't pleased when my sons walked away from the boat a year ago. I didn't understand how Yeshua could say to them, 'Follow me,' and without a backward glance, they did."

He looked toward the lake, almost as if he could see the boat and his sons and Yeshua.

"They were all gone for a time, Yeshua and the twelve he called first. They were in Jerusalem. In Judea. Even in Samaria. But eventually they returned to Galilee. That was when I began to understand what happened to my sons."

He smiled at Zlata, his eyes lit with excitement.

"There were five of them that day. Yeshua, along with Simon and Andrew, the sons of John, and my two boys. They had been to the synagogue, as had I, and when we left, Simon, the one Yeshua calls Cephas, invited the rabbi and the others, including me, to his home to eat. But when we got there, we learned that Simon's mother-in-law, Elisheva, was sick in bed with a high fever. Simon's wife, Leah, was distraught, thinking her mother might die. She was that ill."

Zlata listened, her heart rate increasing, eager to know what had changed Zebedee's mind about Yeshua but concerned to know what had happened to Simon's mother-in-law as well.

"Yeshua went to Elisheva. He leaned low over the bed, and he spoke to her. I don't know what was said. I was still standing near the door of the house. Then he touched her hand. Even from where I stood, I saw the change in her. She immediately rose from the bed, as healthy as I'd ever seen her. She took charge of the meal preparation, and before any time had passed, she was serving us."

"She must have been better than Leah thought."

"No," Zebedee replied with force. "She was ill unto death. But Yeshua healed her with a touch of his hand, with the sound of his voice."

Could it have happened as Zebedee said? Could Yeshua heal someone with a word or a touch? The rumors of healings, of miracles, had swirled throughout Galilee for over a year. Taneli said they were lies, that people were paid to spread the lies. But this was Zebedee, the friend of her father, saying he had seen it for himself.

"Zlata, Yeshua will return to Capernaum. When he does, make it a point to go to see him, to listen to him. See for yourself."

"You sound like Bilhah," she whispered, more to herself than to Zebedee.

But he heard her. "Bilhah." He smiled again. "Yes, she would tell you much the same thing."

Zlata sat a little straighter. "You heard what happened at Simon the Pharisee's house? You've seen her since that night?"

"I heard. I saw her yesterday in the shop of Jonah the weaver. She is changed. As changed as the woman called Mary who was freed from the seven demons that possessed her."

A chill ran through Zlata. She didn't know what a demon-possessed person looked like. She didn't want to know. But something told her that Zebedee was right. That Bilhah had changed just as much as the woman called Mary.

"See him for yourself, Zlata," Zebedee added as he rose from the bank. "You will see."

Zlata watched as the man strode away, a desire to know the truth for herself taking hold in her heart.

CHAPTER NINE

Several weeks passed. The heat of early summer arrived, blanketing the region.

Taneli kept himself informed of everything Yeshua did or said as the young rabbi continued to travel about the countryside, teaching in synagogues and on hillsides. Word of the teacher's miracles continued to spread. More and more people from throughout Galilee and beyond came to Capernaum in search of Yeshua. Taneli railed to his friends about the various laws the Nazarene had broken, and among themselves they tried to devise ways that would destroy his popularity with the people.

As for Zlata, the encouragement of both Bilhah and Zebedee to seek out the rabbi to hear him for herself wouldn't leave her alone. She remembered their words when she awakened in the morning. She thought of them when she lay down in darkness, ready for a night's sleep.

"See him for yourself, Zlata…."

"Hear him…."

"He is so much more than we think…."

Otherwise, the days seemed to meld, one into another, without anything to differentiate them.

Zlata was on her way to the marketplace to buy honey cakes, a favorite of her mother-in-law's, when a crowd on the road leading north drew her attention. Without joining them, there was no way for her to be certain that the people were gathered because of Yeshua. But somehow she was certain anyway.

She should continue on to Capernaum. She should rush to complete her errand for Abra. She should, but she didn't. Instead, her feet carried her toward the crowd.

Murmurs and excited voices reached her well before she arrived. Taller men and women blocked her view, so she moved up a gentle rise on the right side of the road. From there, she saw Yeshua as he leaned down to touch the head of someone seated on the side of the road. Adjusting her position a little more, she saw who was on the ground. Even after so many years, she recognized him. It was Hevel, a young man of the town, the son of a fisherman who had worked with her father. Hevel was a mute. He'd been unable to make a sound since birth.

Zlata had been a girl of seven or eight when Hevel was born, a few houses down from her own, and she'd seen him often in the street as he'd grown up. Other children had teased and picked on him unmercifully whenever he tried to join them in their games. She remembered well the frustration and sadness that had been written on his face. He'd wanted to communicate with others but couldn't do anything but wave his hands and arms and move his mouth without a sound.

"Be kind to him, Zlata," her mother had said. "He is a good boy. The other children are mean only because they don't understand. Perhaps they are afraid that something like it could happen to them."

"What sin did his parents do so that Hevel was born mute?" she had asked.

Her mother had shaken her head. "I don't know. I don't understand the ways of God. I don't know why some prosper and others falter, why one man is strong and another weak. I only know we should be kind to our neighbors."

Zlata had done her best to honor her mother's wishes, going out of her way to help and protect the mute boy whenever she could. But then she had married and moved away. After her parents died, she hadn't seen Hevel again, for she no longer went to the part of Capernaum where they'd lived. The reminders hurt too much.

Now, there he was. Not the boy she'd remembered but a young man. A young man who still couldn't communicate, from the look of it. A young man who probably lived with his parents or else had to beg in order to survive.

Yeshua, with his hand still resting upon Hevel's head, said something that Zlata couldn't hear.

She saw tears fill the young man's eyes. And then, in a voice that was deep and ragged, he said, "Thank you…Master."

Zlata gasped. So did those around her. Someone near her cried, "He's cast out a demon!" Someone else responded, "He does so by Beelzebul! Away with him. Away with them both." From across the road, another shouted, "Lord, give us a sign from heaven!"

Yeshua straightened. His intense gaze swept the crowd. When he spoke, it was with an equally intense voice. "Any kingdom divided against itself is laid waste; and a house divided against itself falls. If Satan also is divided against himself, how will his kingdom stand?"

Zlata realized she held her breath, not wanting to miss a single syllable. She forced herself to inhale and release it.

"For you say that I cast out demons by Beelzebul," Yeshua continued as he turned in a slow circle. "And if I by Beelzebul cast out demons, by whom do your sons cast them out? So they will be your judges. But if I cast out demons by the finger of God, then the kingdom of God has come upon you."

The kingdom of God has come upon you? Zlata frowned. What did that mean?

"Yeshua can show you the way," Bilhah had told her. *"He will show you what the kingdom of God is like...."*

Zlata's heart quickened in her chest. *Show me. I want to see. I want to understand. Show me....*

"He who is not with Me is against Me; and he who does not gather with Me, scatters."

She closed her eyes for a moment.

I don't understand.

She opened her eyes and found Yeshua looking straight at her, just as he had done at Simon's house. Her heart nearly stopped.

A woman in the crowd called out, "Blessed is the womb that bore You and the breasts at which You nursed."

Yeshua's gaze moved on from Zlata, and he answered, "On the contrary, blessed are those who hear the word of God and observe it." He looked at Hevel again and offered his hand, then drew the young man to his feet. "Blessed are those who hear the word of God and observe it," he repeated, more softly this time.

"I will, Lord," Hevel said, his voice still gruff sounding. "I hear and I will observe it."

Yeshua began walking, and the crowd parted enough for him and his disciples to pass through. Occasionally, he reached out to touch someone, speaking to them. Many who had surrounded him continued to follow him down the road. Some turned and hurried toward the town gates, no doubt to tell others what they had seen. Soon, only Zlata remained. Or so she thought until she turned and saw Hevel, once again sitting on the ground.

"Hevel?" She stepped down to the road.

He looked at her. A frown wrinkled his forehead for a moment. Then his eyes widened in recognition. "Zlata? The daughter of Ira?" He rose and stepped forward.

"Yes."

He touched his throat, then his lips. "I can speak."

"I know. I saw and heard." She gave her head a small shake. "What did he do? What did he say to you?"

"He put his hand on my head and said, almost too soft for me to hear, 'Be whole.' And I felt…I felt something go out of me."

"*What* went out of you?"

"I don't know." He stared up the road where stragglers could still be seen. "All I know is that I've never spoken, could never speak, and now I can." A grin split his face. "I must go. I must find my father and tell him what has happened." Without a backward glance, he took off in the direction of the lake, running as fast as his legs could carry him.

What would her father-in-law say when he heard about Yeshua and Hevel? Undoubtedly he would agree with the person who'd said the demon was cast out by Beelzebul. Or he would again insist that this had all been pretense, that someone had paid a healthy person to pretend to be mute. But Taneli would be wrong. She knew Hevel. She'd observed his silence since birth. She'd seen this miracle with her own eyes. It was a miracle, and there was nothing evil in it. The moment was…blessed.

"Blessed are those who hear the word of God and observe it."

She would see Yeshua again. She would listen to him as Bilhah had said she should do. Nothing would be able to keep her from it.

CHAPTER TEN

Several days later, Zlata slipped away from the house. She'd heard from one of the other servants that Yeshua was walking on the road near Taneli's vineyards earlier in the day, but by the time she arrived, she found the road silent and mostly deserted. There was no sign of the crowds that were said to follow the teacher everywhere. Disappointment washed over her. Perhaps if she had been able to get away sooner… But there had been too many chores to do.

Reluctant to return to the house, she sank to the ground near a large sycamore tree. The shade provided a pleasant respite from the heat of the day. After a few moments, she lay back on the ground and stared up through the large limbs of the old tree. Clouds dotted the blue of the sky. The clouds were as still as she was. Languid. Sleepy. So warm.

Her eyes drifted closed.

She dreamed of the sea, of the sun glimmering across its surface. She saw her father standing in his fishing boat. His upper arms bulged with strength as he flung the net into the water. He grinned when the net began to scoop up fish. This was to be a good day on the Sea of Galilee, and she was on the boat to witness it. She heard laughter and felt joy welling up from deep within. Her father reached out, tenderly touching her cheek. She could almost hear him speak to her. She could almost hear his voice above the wind in the sail and the waves lapping against the boat. She could almost…

Her eyes opened, and a man's face above her came into focus. With a squeal of surprise, she sat upright.

Joel, the steward, backed away, his arms outstretched, his palms toward her. "It's all right, Zlata. It's only me. I saw you on the ground and wanted to make sure you were all right."

"I–I'm fine." She scrambled to her feet. "I was…resting." She swept her hands down her tunic, brushing away dirt and grass. Then she made certain her headscarf was in place.

An amused expression crossed Joel's face. Was he laughing at her?

Zlata huffed out a breath. "I must go back."

"I'll walk with you as far as the turnoff."

"It isn't necessary."

"But I'm going that way already."

"Then, I suppose…" She let the words fade into silence.

As soon as Zlata moved away from the tree, Joel fell into step on her right, a respectful distance separating them. He walked with his head dipped forward, his hands clasped behind his back. Although she glanced over at him several times, she never saw him look her way. But he seemed to be wearing that amused expression again, and it—along with his silence—angered her. He had no right to laugh at her.

They had nearly reached the turnoff to the vineyard when he spoke again. "Were you hoping to see Yeshua?"

She looked over at him.

"He is…compelling," Joel added.

"You've heard him teach?"

He nodded. "Once. When he was teaching near the vineyard. I slipped away and listened. He has a way of teaching…." He ended with a shrug.

"I—I was present when he healed Hevel the mute."

"You were there? You actually saw it happen?" Joel stopped walking. Amazement filled his eyes.

Zlata stopped as well and turned to face him. "I was there. I saw it." She glanced up the road, then down it. "I heard Hevel speak. The first words he said in his life. I heard them."

"Tell me about it. Please."

She didn't know if she should. Taneli wanted to quash all talk about the young rabbi from Nazareth. And yet she longed to share what she had seen and heard with someone. She couldn't do so within Taneli's household. But here was Joel, asking her to share. He found the teacher compelling. Would it be so wrong to answer his questions, to tell him what she had seen?

She complied at last, the words almost tumbling out of her once she gave herself permission. Speaking about Hevel's healing aloud, her heart was stirred all over again. Her amazement was just as profound as the moment it had happened.

"I must look for Hevel when I go to the market." Joel's gaze moved in the direction of town. "I would like to see him, to talk to him. I would like him to tell me what it felt like, how his parents reacted."

Emboldened, Zlata decided to tell Joel about the dinner at Simon's house. About the way Yeshua had spoken about forgiveness. About the transformation of Bilhah.

Joel listened in silence, and when she was finished, he said, "Who is this man that he can forgive sins?"

"I don't know," she whispered. "I asked myself that same question when it happened." In her mind, she heard her father-in-law's rants against Yeshua, and a chill shivered through her. Despite it, she added, "I don't know who he is, but I want to know."

"So do I."

Strange. She'd disliked Joel ever since he'd benefited from her husband's murder. Now she felt connected to him because of Yeshua. They both wanted to know how he could heal a young man with a mere touch or a few words. And then there was what Yeshua had done for Bilhah. There was such a change in her. Not simply that she was no longer living a life of degradation in order to survive. No, something had changed *within* Bilhah. Zlata had witnessed it.

Joel took a step back from her. "I'd better go. I have work to do."

"Yes. I must return to my work too." She mirrored his step backward.

With a smile and a small wave, Joel turned and hurried up the road to the vineyard. Zlata watched him go, wondering how one brief encounter could change how she felt about a person. Then she too turned and went on her way.

"Where have you been?" Dara whispered urgently when she saw Zlata slip through the courtyard door.

"I went for a walk." It wasn't a good explanation, but it was all she had.

"The master asked for you. He was very upset when you couldn't be found."

Zlata's pulse skittered. "Where is he?" She glanced toward the door to the main room of the house.

"He left with Nathan."

"I'll see if Abra needs me."

"She's gone to see her sister."

Zlata calmed slightly. "Then I will return to the sewing."

"The master won't forget that you were gone without explanation."

"I know." She tucked her head and hurried into the house.

She was still seated on a stool, sewing another new tunic for Abra, when she heard Taneli's voice from the courtyard. Sweat trickled down her spine, more from nerves than from the heat of the afternoon.

"Zlata!"

She set the linen aside and hurried to answer the call.

Stepping through the doorway, she said, "Yes, my lord." She kept her gaze on the ground.

"You were seen with him." The words were soft but filled with anger.

Confused, she shook her head. Why would it matter if she was seen with Joel? Taneli himself had sent her with messages for the steward numerous times over the years. Was it because they had been together on a public road rather than on the grounds of the vineyard? Perhaps. But who could have reported the meeting before she arrived at the house? Taneli had been upset when he left the house, according to Dara. He couldn't have known that Zlata and Joel had been on the road together.

"You were seen with the Nazarene." Taneli seemed to grind out the words.

"With the Nazarene?" She looked up, her thoughts scrambling to change direction.

Taneli slapped her with the back of his hand, and she slammed against the wall of the house. Pain shot down her arm and up her neck. Her cheek throbbed.

"You will not become part of the rabble that follows him."

"I—I wasn't. I—I didn't."

"Do not lie to me."

Tears made his visage swim before her as she covered her cheek with her hand.

"Do not lie," he warned again.

She lowered her gaze. "My lord, I was on my way to buy something for my mistress. I saw all the people. I tried to see what was happening. That is all. Yeshua moved on without saying more than a few words in my hearing. I did not follow him. I went straight to the marketplace."

"Blessed are those who hear the word of God and observe it."

She'd told the truth. Yeshua had said little, but what he'd said had touched her heart in a way she didn't understand and couldn't have explained, even if she'd dared.

"You will not shame me, Zlata. Do you understand?"

"I understand, my lord."

"Return to your chores."

She scurried away without response.

"Zlata," Dara called to her.

She shook her head and kept moving.

All these years, her father-in-law had seldom spoken to her except to criticize or shame her. She was a woman, which was bad enough. But worse still, she hadn't moved out of a Roman soldier's way in time, and so Taneli's beloved son had died. Then she'd been unable to keep her only child alive. He disliked her, even despised her, and she'd learned it was in her best interests when he didn't notice her at all.

But now he had taken note that she'd been in the vicinity of Yeshua the Nazarene, and that had earned her his wrath.

She sank onto the stool in the corner and let herself weep, feeling again the moment his hand had connected with her face, feeling the pain in her shoulder where she had hit the wall. So different from the gentle touch of her father in her dream. A wave of sorrow washed over her.

Why, God? Why? What have I done?

As if in answer, she remembered the way Yeshua had looked at her. He'd seen her, and he hadn't reacted with disdain. He'd seen her and…and he'd cared. How she knew this she couldn't say, but it was true.

Wiping away her tears, she glanced toward the door. Taneli had told her not to shame him, but he hadn't forbidden her to listen to the teacher. She wasn't to follow Yeshua, but she could listen to him. She *had* to listen. She had to.

CHAPTER ELEVEN

Zlata was sweeping the floor of the rooftop when she heard a rare sound—Taneli's laughter. She set aside the broom, then she walked toward the edge and looked down into the open courtyard where her father-in-law sat with his frequent companion, Nathan the younger.

"They wanted to take him away," Nathan said as he stroked his beard. "Even his own mother and brothers think he's lost his mind. They came to retrieve him, to take him home. That should begin to change people's opinion of him."

"You're right. He'll be forced to leave Capernaum soon. I feel it in my bones." Taneli slapped his hands against his thighs, signaling his pleasure. "The crowds will turn on him. Our success is at hand. Galilee will soon return to normal. Another so-called messiah forgotten."

Zlata took a step back. It wouldn't be good if her father-in-law thought she spied on him, especially not when he was talking about the young rabbi. Unless Taneli addressed her, he believed his business was none of hers. True enough. But news of Yeshua concerned her. She touched her cheek. It concerned her now more than ever.

She retrieved the broom and began sweeping again, her thoughts in turmoil. Nearly two weeks had passed since Taneli had forbidden her to follow Yeshua. In that time, except for fetching water from the well and buying produce and fish in the marketplace, her duties had kept her close to the house. But if Taneli was right, she might not have many remaining opportunities to see and hear the rabbi speak. She couldn't bear the thought of that. She *needed* to see him again. She would have to pay more attention to the gossip about the teacher when she was in the marketplace or at the well. She simply needed reasons to be away from the house, tasks that required extra time. But what could that possibly be? She didn't know. She couldn't think.

Adonai, help me see the teacher again. Help me to understand what he says.

Zlata's prayer was answered later that very morning. She was sent with a message to Abra's cousin, Keziah, who lived in Bethsaida. Zlata had made the walk many times over the years. A healthy young person could cover the distance in little more than an hour. It usually took Zlata longer because she took pleasure in looking at the hills on one side and the sea on the other and so was in no hurry.

But today it wasn't the view that slowed her journey. Today the road to Bethsaida was clogged with people, most of them walking fast, some even running. She didn't need to be told why. She knew. Her pulse quickened, as did her own footsteps.

She was more than halfway to her destination when a rise in the road that followed the shore of the lake allowed her to glimpse the Nazarene in his simple tunic. People filled the shore and the ground overlooking the lake. She saw Yeshua step into a fishing boat and some of his disciples push it into deeper water.

Zlata glanced around, suddenly wondering who might have seen her on the day of Hevel's healing. Seen her and then reported it to Taneli. It wouldn't be good for her if that should happen again, even though she couldn't have avoided passing by this place. She had to in order to complete the errand.

Pulling her scarf down on her forehead, she dipped her head down and tried to avoid drawing the attention of others as she looked for a place to sit, a spot where she could see the rabbi clearly and, hopefully, hear whatever he had to say.

"Zlata."

She recognized Joel's voice even before she found him with her eyes. Her pulse quickened. He wasn't far from her. He hadn't spoken too loudly. She could only hope everyone else was so focused on the teacher that they hadn't heard him too.

"Here." He held out an arm. "Join me. You can see from here."

Joel had claimed a position on a large, flat-topped rock, giving him a superior view. She moved toward him, accepting his hand so he could pull her up beside him. Then they sat, their gazes turned down to the boat and to Yeshua.

As if sensing the teacher was about to speak, the multitude quieted. All that could be heard was the lapping of water on the shore and the whisper of a warm breeze.

"Listen to this!" Yeshua's voice carried to them, almost as if he were no more than a few steps away. "Behold, the sower went out to sow; as he was sowing, some seed fell beside the road, and the birds came and ate it up."

Zlata drew a deep breath, trying to quiet the racing of her heart, trying to take in what he said.

"Other seed fell on the rocky ground where it did not have much soil; and immediately it sprang up because it had no depth of soil. And after the sun had risen, it was scorched; and because it had no root, it withered away."

She leaned forward, certain the words he spoke were important for her, right then, at that very moment.

"Other seed fell among the thorns, and the thorns came up and choked it, and it yielded no crop." Yeshua's gaze moved across the crowd, lingering here and there.

Would he see her? Would he know she was present once again? Would he know that she longed to hear and understand, that she had prayed for this opportunity?

"Other seeds fell into the good soil, and as they grew up and increased, they yielded a crop and produced thirty, sixty, and a hundredfold."

How strange, she thought. The first time she'd heard Yeshua speak, his words had made her angry. She'd left the crowd after listening only a short while. She'd agreed with Taneli. She'd thought Yeshua crazy, a madman. She'd disagreed with him, had even felt wounded by his words.

"He who has ears to hear, let him hear."

I'm listening, Yeshua. I hear you.

Somehow, even as she leaned in to learn more from the teacher, she became aware of the passage of time. It seemed no more than a minute since she'd sank onto this rock beside Joel. But it had been more. Much more.

She looked at Joel. "I must go," she said softly.

"Not yet. Not while Yeshua is still speaking."

"I must. Taneli would not like—"

The steward nodded with understanding. "Yes." He stood, then helped her rise as well.

Zlata tugged her scarf forward once again, trying to hide her face from any prying eyes. Then she followed Joel away from the lake and the boat and Yeshua.

It seemed to take forever before they broke through the multitude. A mostly empty road lay before her. A few people hurried toward them, wanting to join the throng. A few others were headed away, for whatever reason not staying to hear more. Perhaps, like Zlata, there was somewhere they had to be. Or perhaps, like the first time she'd heard the teacher, they didn't understand and couldn't believe.

She felt her eyes widen. *I didn't have ears to hear.* She glanced behind her. *But now I do.*

"Do you need me to go with you?" Joel asked, drawing her gaze to him.

"No. Thank you. It is better you do not. You...you have been kind to me, Joel."

A slight smile tipped the corners of his mouth. "That's easy to do, Zlata."

Heat rose in her cheeks. She dipped her eyes and hurried on her way, walking swiftly, almost running. Only when the crowd was far behind her did she allow herself to slow a bit. As her breathing also slowed, she heard the words of Yeshua again. The sower. The seeds on rocky ground. The scorched seeds. The seeds among the thorns. The good soil, yielding a large crop.

"He who has ears to hear, let him hear."

She chewed her lower lip as she walked. In her heart, she knew Yeshua didn't tell stories simply to tell stories. He didn't care about entertaining the people. He spoke with a purpose.

El Shaddai, help me understand the meaning behind the parables.

She replayed the words she'd heard again, even slower this time, and had just reached the part about a yield of thirty, sixty, and a hundredfold when Keziah's house at the edge of Bethsaida came into view. For a moment, Zlata couldn't remember the message she'd been sent to deliver. Panic tightened her chest. But by the time she reached the door, she'd recalled Abra's instructions and was able to give the message to Keziah exactly as it had been given to her.

Keziah invited her to sit and have a bite to eat and something to drink. Realizing the older woman desired company, Zlata obliged. Perhaps it was self-serving, but she also realized staying for a while would give her an excuse for her lengthy absence, should Taneli question her later.

After washing the dust from her feet, Zlata sat near Keziah, and the two women shared a meal of bread, goat cheese, fruit, and wine. As they ate, Keziah asked about the new tunics Zlata had made for her cousin. She knew how much Abra liked fine clothing. She asked if Taneli had any news of interest from the

Holy City. She asked about old friends who lived in Capernaum and recounted a few stories of her own from her childhood there.

Zlata listened much more than she talked, and when she left Bethsaida an hour later, she felt as if she was leaving a friend.

CHAPTER TWELVE

Zlata hadn't attended synagogue on a regular basis in many years. Her sorrow and bitterness had been too great. When she went, she didn't accompany Taneli and Abra. She no longer felt a part of their family, as she had been when Yerik was alive. Her in-laws offered her shelter, food, and work. Nothing more.

But when she awakened on the next Sabbath morning, she knew she wanted to go to the service. She wanted to hear the readings from the Torah. Yeshua's story of the sower had kept churning in her mind ever since that day by the lake, and something about it had made her hungry to hear the scripture read and taught. She wanted to hear and recite the familiar prayers. Perhaps then she would understand more this time than she ever had before.

Zlata owned one nice headscarf, a gift from her parents. She'd taken special care with the deep blue linen through the years. It was precious to her. She donned it today, covering her forehead and dark hair, then made her way to the Capernaum synagogue. Once there, she sat on a wooden bench against the wall nearest the entrance. She spied her father-in-law at the opposite end of the spacious room, close to the Moses seat. Taneli often sat there to teach on the Sabbath. At the moment, her father-in-law wore a particularly dark expression. She followed his gaze and realized why. Yeshua was present in the synagogue, along with many of his disciples.

Her heart quickened. She'd heard that he had read from the Torah in this synagogue in the past year, but it hadn't been on a Sabbath when Zlata was present. Would he do so today?

"Blessed be You, O Lord, King of the world, who forms the light and creates the darkness, who makes peace and creates everything."

So began the ancient benediction, announcing the start of the morning assembly. But try as she might, Zlata couldn't look away from Yeshua. There was a serenity that surrounded him, and she wished she understood it.

"Hear, O Israel! The Lord our God is one Lord."

She didn't know who sat in the Moses seat. She scarcely heard the words read from the scroll. What she noted was Yeshua's posture and the expression on his face. He had a great reverence for the law, a great love for Adonai. She knew it in the marrow of her being. Why couldn't everyone see it as clearly as she did?

Someone else read from the scroll, and still she didn't hear the words. Instead, she sorted through everything she'd ever heard about the Nazarene, both before and after he came to stay in Capernaum. She allowed the four times she'd seen him with her own eyes to replay in her mind—the words she'd heard him speak to sink deeper into her heart.

Then he stood, and she caught her breath. Her gaze shot toward Taneli, who glowered at the teacher as he took his place on the wooden dais in the center of the room. Yeshua looked down at the scroll. He didn't seem to read the words when he spoke. But it was more than mere memorization, which most Jewish boys and men could do. And many women too. No, Yeshua seemed to know the words in an even more intimate way.

"Then the Lord said, 'Because this people draw near with their words and honor Me with their lip service, but they remove their hearts far from Me, and their reverence for Me consists of tradition learned by rote.'"

Yeshua kept reading, but Zlata's attention remained on the opening. The words from the prophet Isaiah pierced her heart. Had she drawn near to God with words and lip service but removed her heart from Him? Tears blurred her eyes. The answer was worse than a yes or a no. She hadn't drawn near to the God of Israel at all. She'd felt deserted by Him, and so she had withdrawn from Him in her heart, mind, and spirit. She had turned her back to Him.

Forgive me.

Her parents had raised her to observe the law and to love the Lord. Her husband had lived righteously in all his ways and would have raised his children to do the same. In losing all of them, Zlata had lost her anchor as well. Bitterness, sadness, and fear had taken up residence in her heart, leaving no room for Adonai. Yeshua had forgiven Bilhah for her sins, which were many. Would he also forgive her if he knew how far she'd strayed from the Lord Almighty?

As discreetly as possible, she wiped the tears from her cheeks, and she was the first to slip out of the synagogue when the morning assembly came to an end. She all but ran down the narrow street and out of Capernaum.

There was no need to hurry back to the house, of course. No one cooked on the Sabbath. They would eat what had been prepared the day before. Everyone in the household, master and servants alike, would rest. If Zlata chose to slip away, this was the one day she would need no excuse in order to do so.

Her footsteps slowed. She glanced behind her. The road was empty for the moment. Taneli and Abra were usually among the last to leave the synagogue. Others would want to stop Taneli, to ask him questions about the law, and he would want to answer them in great detail. Taneli loved the attention and the praise of others.

She thought how people crowded around Yeshua. How they followed him. How they reached out to touch his garments. She thought how he looked at others. His gaze could be intense or compassionate. Sometimes it was both at the same time. And always—always—he looked at people with love. Even from a distance, she'd seen that in his eyes. She'd heard that the teacher often went into the hills to be alone and to pray. He had no home of his own. He stayed with others in Capernaum and perhaps made camp in the hills when he wasn't teaching in other villages and towns in the region. These days, large groups followed him everywhere.

Zlata had no physical sickness for Yeshua to cure. Her legs were straight. Her hands worked. She could see, hear, and speak. But there had long been a sickness in her heart. Could Yeshua heal that too? Would he?

Yes. The truth rushed through her like a flood. Yes. He could and He would.

How did she know? How could she be so certain? Because of who He was. Yeshua *was* the Messiah. Only the Messiah could do what Yeshua had done. How could she not have understood that before today?

Taneli could strike her. He could threaten her. But it wouldn't change what she knew to be true.

Yeshua was the long awaited one.

The Messiah.

CHAPTER THIRTEEN

It was early in the morning, on the second day of the week, when Zlata knelt in the straw beside the foal that had been born to one of Taneli's donkeys. Slowly, so as not to frighten him, she reached out to stroke his muzzle. It was soft and warm beneath her fingertips.

"Good work," she said to the jenny who observed her. "You have a fine son."

One of the donkey's ears cocked forward, as if in agreement. The foal moved away from Zlata, nuzzling his mother, searching for breakfast.

For a moment, Zlata remembered what it was like to hold an infant to her breast, to breathe in the sweet scent of her son as she cradled him in her arms. She remembered the love for Uriah that had rushed through her at times, overwhelmed her, consumed her. But such memories were nothing but ruthless foes, teasing her with what was, what might have been, and what would never be again. She tried to push the cruel memories away as she stood and reclaimed the water jar. With hurried steps, she walked toward the well in town.

She'd left the house earlier than usual, and no other women were congregated around the cistern yet. She filled the jar with water then placed it on a nearby stone and sat beside it, in no hurry to return to the house. She'd been shut up inside much of the previous day when an unexpected storm had rolled through. Black clouds, high winds, and drenching rain had made the day miserable for farmers, travelers, and fishermen alike.

Yerik, had he been living, would have rushed to the rooftop to watch as the squall stirred up waves upon the lake. He would have delighted in the flashes of lightning and the sound of the thunder rolling across the heavens. He wouldn't have minded being soaked by rain. He probably would have laughed at it.

Zlata shook her head. That was twice this morning she'd allowed her thoughts to go back in time. Hadn't she learned how harmful that was?

And yet…

She sat up straighter, analyzing her feelings. While the memories reminded her how much she missed her husband and baby, tears had not followed either time. Even more, neither had the usual bitterness. How odd. How strange. How—

"Good morning, Zlata."

She looked up to see Channah approach. Simon's servant carried her own water jar.

"Good morning," Zlata replied.

"It's going to be a beautiful day."

Zlata's gaze rose to the clear blue sky. "Yes. And hot, no doubt."

More voices carried to them as other women neared the well. More greetings were exchanged. More remarks about the weather, especially the previous day's unexpected storm.

Zlata was only half listening when a comment caught her attention.

"Yeshua calmed the sea with a command, and it obeyed Him."

Slowly, silence blanketed the gathering of women.

Then someone said, "Rebekah, tell us more. What did your husband tell you?"

"Yeshua and His disciples were in a boat, sailing to the other side of the lake. Then that storm blew in." Rebekah spoke in an excited but soft voice, forcing others to lean in. "Yeshua fell asleep, but the men with Him were fighting to keep the boat afloat in the fierce gale. They were being swamped with the raging water. But Yeshua slept through it all."

"How could He? How could anyone sleep in a boat in a storm like that one? The thunder rattled my bones."

"I don't know," Rebekah answered sharply. "But that's what I was told. My husband was at the lake. He should know."

"Go on with your story," someone else said.

Rebekah was quick to comply. "His men called out to wake Him. 'Master, we are perishing!' They were terrified. Wouldn't you be?" She looked at the women around her. "They were certain they would all drown before it was over. One of them asked Yeshua if He didn't care that they were about to die."

Zlata couldn't be certain about the other women around the well, but she was hanging on Rebekah's every word. Her pulse raced, and her breathing was shallow.

"Awakened at last, Yeshua got up. Then He rebuked the wind and surging waves."

"Rebuked?"

Rebekah lifted her chin, her voice growing more dramatic. "He called out, 'Hush, be still.' And the wind instantly died down, and the sea became perfectly calm."

"Jeremiah saw how suddenly it quieted on the lake yesterday. He told me all about it. He's never seen anything like it. That's what he said. It must be true."

"And then," Rebekah added as if the other woman hadn't spoken, "Yeshua looked at His disciples and asked them why they were afraid. 'Do you still have no faith?' He asked them."

Murmurs passed among the listeners.

Rebekah turned and her gaze met briefly with Zlata's as she continued, "'Who then is this,' they asked, 'that even the wind and the sea obey Him?'"

It seemed for a moment that Zlata's heart ceased to beat. Because she knew the answer. She wanted to shout the answer.

Who then is this that even the wind and sea obey Him? He is the Messiah, the Anointed One.

It amazed her that His disciples, who had lived with Him and talked with Him and walked with Him for so long now, had asked such a question. Even they had a difficult time believing their own eyes and ears.

Who then is this that even the wind and sea obey Him?

She knew the answer, and joy exploded within as she rose and put the water jar on her shoulder. With a hasty nod and a few words of farewell, she started back to Taneli's house.

Who is this Man?

Yeshua wasn't a madman as she'd once thought Him, as Taneli still believed Him to be. Yeshua had the authority to cast out demons and to heal the lepers, the blind, the lame. He had the power to forgive sins. He had given a voice to Hevel. And now He'd calmed the storm with just a word. No ordinary man could do such things. Yeshua confounded the Pharisees and scribes. People flocked to Him from all over the region, hoping to be healed of all kinds of diseases. They gathered to hear Him teach, both in the synagogues and on the hillsides.

Who was like Him? No one. No one was like Yeshua the Nazarene.

CHAPTER FOURTEEN

"You are to go and stay with Keziah," Abra told Zlata a few days after the big storm. "She is injured and in need of help until she is able to walk again."

"I'm sorry your cousin is hurt. I will be glad to help her however I can."

"The physician believes it will be some weeks before she can manage on her own. Such a bother, but she has no one else to turn to. Her daughter is far away, and even when she was here, I thought her rather worthless."

Keziah had treated Zlata with kindness whenever they had been together in the years since Yerik's and Uriah's deaths. Going to stay with her would be a pleasant change. Abra didn't mean her cousin's request to be a gift for Zlata, but it was.

She set off for Bethsaida before the sun reached its zenith. It hadn't been quite two weeks since she'd followed this same road, on her way to Keziah's house with a message, and she'd come upon Yeshua teaching by the sea. She'd also happened upon Joel in the crowd.

Part of her wished she would see the steward again. She would like to tell him what she'd seen and heard since their chance meeting. He would be interested in what she'd observed in the synagogue. He would like to hear what had happened on the lake during the storm, if others hadn't carried the story to him already.

Zlata smiled, feeling a lightness of being. Was this happiness? She thought, perhaps, it might be. The emotion had been a stranger to her for so long, it was difficult to be certain.

It's because of Yeshua.

He hadn't touched her and healed a physical illness. He hadn't spoken and forgiven her sins. Yet she couldn't help thinking He was the reason for the way she felt. As if hope had blossomed inside of her. As if light had entered a dark corner of her heart.

Hear, O Israel! The Lord our God is one Lord.

A sudden breeze off the sea caught her head scarf, lifting it, threatening to pull it from her head. If she hadn't been on a public road, she would have been tempted to let it go, to feel the warmth of the sun on her head, to let her long hair fly and flutter as the scarf did now. But good sense prevailed. She grabbed the fabric and tucked it back into place.

After glancing around and seeing no one, she left the road and made her way to the lakeshore. She found a large rock to sit upon, removed her sandals, and dipped her feet into the water. Far out from where she sat, she saw some boats.

As a little girl, she'd loved those times when she and her mother had come to the lake with her father early in the morning. She'd loved to watch him and the other fishermen push their boats out into the lake, to see the hoisted sails flapping against the blue sky, to hear oars slapping the water. She'd loved the shore and the sand and the rocks. She'd loved the sun warming her skin. And when her father returned home at night, she'd never minded the fishy smell that had clung to him. To her, it was a scent mingled with love.

She smiled again. The scent of love. Yerik had often smelled of the earth and the grapes. It was more difficult to define than the smell of fish but real to her all the same. And so sweet and comforting in her memories today.

With her arms braced on the rock, she leaned back and turned her face to the sun, eyes closed. Memories that were comforting. All these years, her memories had reminded her of what had been lost. They'd brought tears. They'd made her bitter. When had it changed? How had it changed?

But, of course, she already knew the answer to those questions. Just as Yeshua was the reason for her ability to feel happy again, this slow change had begun when she first went to listen to Him. He'd made her both sad and angry with His words that day on the hillside, but all the same, that was the moment the change had begun. She didn't fully understand it, yet she was thankful for it.

She swiveled on the rock, dried her feet with the hem of her tunic, and put on her sandals. Then she set off once again toward Bethsaida. The opening words of the Shema whispered again in her mind: *"Hear, O Israel! The Lord our God is one Lord."*

From her father's knee, she'd learned to repeat the Shema twice daily, a reminder of her commitment to Adonai. But for the first time in years, the words meant something to her. Yeshua had opened her heart so that it might be so.

Her spirits remained high all the way to Keziah's home.

She found Abra's cousin seated outside in the shade, the breeze from the lake providing occasional relief from the heat of the afternoon. Her right foot was braced on a wooden stool. Her eyes were closed, and the expression on her face was one of pain.

"Keziah," Zlata called softly.

Her eyes opened. "Zlata! Abra sent you."

"Yes. I'm to stay until you are able to walk again."

"I can walk a little now. But only in and out of the house. I can't go to the market or the well. That's too far."

Zlata knelt on the ground near the stool. "What did you do?"

"I fell." The older woman inched her tunic out of the way, revealing an ugly wound. "I tripped climbing some stone steps. It was very clumsy of me and happened fast. I fell forward and then I slid down." The skin had been scraped off a large section of Keziah's leg, from the top of her foot up to her knee, and the ankle was swollen and red.

"Oh, Keziah. I am sorry."

"It was good of Abra to let you come to me."

Like Zlata, Keziah was a widow. Her only child, a daughter, had married and resettled in Jerusalem. According to Abra, Keziah had been asked to come live with them, but she hadn't wanted to leave the home she'd lived in all her life, first with her parents, then with her husband and child. And so she remained here alone, without even a servant to attend to her, since her purse didn't allow for such a luxury.

"What do you need me to do first?" Zlata asked as she rose to her feet.

"Fill the water jar, I think. A neighbor brought some vegetables and bread for my supper."

"I will go at once. You rest, and I will return soon."

Zlata had a difficult time trying to fall asleep that night. Perhaps it was the sighs and groans coming from Keziah on the next sleeping mat or perhaps it was the heat that lingered in the small house, even after nighttime had blanketed the earth.

Finally, Zlata rose. Taking her blanket with her, she went outside and climbed the ladder up to the roof. Moonlight glanced off the surface of the lake, making it feel almost as bright as day. The water was like glass tonight, and the sky overhead glittered with stars. No storm. No wind. No rain. Nothing like several days before.

She wondered where Yeshua slept tonight. Was He in the home of a friend in Capernaum? Was He camping under the stars, looking up at the same night sky that she was? As Messiah, did He know how many stars there were? He seemed to know many other things. Why not that?

"The foxes have holes," Yeshua had told one scribe, according to Taneli, *"and the birds of the air have nests, but the Son of Man has nowhere to lay His head."*

Perhaps that was why men like her father-in-law couldn't recognize the Messiah when they saw Him. They expected

Him to come in wealth and power, in charge of an army. Yeshua didn't even have a home or a bed of His own. He was not what anyone in Israel expected.

"El Shaddai, protect Yeshua wherever He is. Keep Him from danger. Don't let the Romans or men like Taneli harm Him. He seems to go about unafraid, but I am afraid for Him. And I'm afraid for myself because…because I believe in Him."

A breeze off the lake caressed her cheek.

I'm always afraid of something, aren't I?

The silent confession made her heart ache. It shamed her. She hadn't been a fearful child. In fact, her mother had often begged her to take more care. So when had it begun? She supposed on the road to Magdala where Yerik had been slain. Or perhaps it had started not long after she was widowed, when she'd realized she was completely alone and unloved.

She saw Him then, in her mind, the rabbi from Nazareth. She saw that particular smile that Yeshua so often wore when He looked at those around Him. She saw the compassion and the intensity of His gaze. And she felt…she felt His love for her. She was no one. She wasn't even one of His disciples. The few times she'd seen Him, heard Him, had been brief. And yet… and yet she knew that He loved her, that she was special to Him. Knowing it changed her in some way she couldn't define.

"And still I'm afraid," she whispered into the moonlit night. "How do I stop being afraid?"

CHAPTER FIFTEEN

Zlata pushed loose strands of hair from her face, then placed the bread dough into the earthen oven to bake. A vegetable stew had begun to simmer over the fire. It would be ready for that night's supper. With no more meal preparations to make, she moved away from the sources of heat, trying to find some relief. There was little to be found, for the morning was already warm.

"Is there anything you need?" she asked Keziah.

As was the case most days, the older woman sat in the shade on the side of the small house, her injured leg on the stool, her eyes closed. "No," Keziah answered without looking. "I need only to rest."

Zlata smiled to herself. Over two weeks had passed since she arrived in Bethsaida, and while Abra's cousin's leg still bore evidence of her nasty fall, Zlata suspected she was better than she made out. Other than caring for her own most personal needs, she'd lifted nary a finger since Zlata came to stay with her. It was obvious she liked both the attention and the company. Zlata could have told Keziah that she was in no hurry to return to Taneli's home. Her daily chores were much the same in both households, but her treatment was better in this place. In truth, Keziah was fond of her. A pleasant change.

"Hello! Zlata!"

Her pulse skipped a beat, and she turned to see Joel walking toward her on the road, his arm raised in a wave.

"Who is that?" Keziah inquired, straightening on her cushion.

"His name is Joel. He's the steward of Taneli's vineyards."

"Do you know him well?"

"No." She shaded her eyes with one hand. "But he worked with Yerik for a long time. My husband respected him and thought he showed great promise."

"Yerik was a good judge of character."

"Yes," Zlata answered softly. "He was." Silently, she added, *Much better than I, it seems. Yerik always liked Joel, but I didn't...at first.*

Joel drew closer to the low stone wall that separated Keziah's house from the road and formed her small courtyard. "I heard you were staying in Bethsaida for a while."

"Yes."

"I didn't know if I would find you, though I hoped I would." His smile was warm. Warmer even than the sun. "But here you are. Standing where I could see you from the road."

"Come in, young man," Keziah called from behind Zlata.

Pleasure seemed to sparkle in his dark eyes. "Thank you."

Zlata turned and led the way to Abra's cousin. Quickly, she introduced them.

"Sit." Keziah pointed to another stool. "You must be thirsty from your long walk." She glanced at Zlata.

"I'll get some water," she said and hurried away.

Returning a couple of minutes later, she found Keziah and Joel in easy conversation. She handed the cup of water to their guest without comment.

"Zlata brings back no news when she goes to the market or the well," Keziah complained, although her smile weakened the chastisement.

"What would you like to know?" Joel asked, leaning back against the house. "Perhaps I can tell you what Zlata hasn't."

Keziah chuckled. "I doubt you would know the kind of gossip I seek."

"Probably not." Joel grinned, his eyes moving to Zlata as she sat on the stone wall across from him.

"Oh, I know." Keziah's face brightened. "What can you tell me of Yeshua, the teacher from Nazareth? I believe He's spent a great deal of time over in Capernaum and around it. You must know something of Him."

Zlata's gaze shot to Keziah, and her heart began to race. Never once over the past two weeks had Keziah mentioned the rabbi. Why had she asked Joel but not Zlata?

Keziah continued, "Some of His first disciples come from this village. Two brothers. Let me see." She frowned in thought. "Oh, yes. Their names are Simon and Andrew. They are fishermen, the sons of Jonah. There's another one too. Not a brother. Hmm. Can't think of his name, but it will come to me."

"I've seen them." Joel rubbed his jaw. "The brothers."

Keziah waved her hand. "It isn't them I want to hear about. Tell me about Yeshua. What have you seen or heard of Him?"

Joel seemed only too happy to comply. He shared several stories, stories that were new to Zlata. A demoniac in Gerasenes, on the eastern shore of Galilee, had been restored to his right mind. A woman who'd suffered a hemorrhage for twelve years had been healed after simply touching the hem of Yeshua's tunic as He'd made His way through a dense crowd. But even more miraculous was the story of Jairus, an official of the synagogue in Capernaum, who had been part of that same crowd. He'd fallen at the feet of Yeshua and implored Him to come to his house where his young daughter lay dying.

"But even as they spoke," Joel said, "someone came from the house of Jairus and told him that his daughter was already dead, so he need not trouble the teacher anymore. Yeshua looked at Jairus and said, 'Do not be afraid any longer; only believe, and she will be made well.'"

"Do not be afraid any longer. Only believe."

The words reverberated inside Zlata.

"Do not be afraid any longer. Only believe."

Joel continued with his story. "Then Yeshua and Jairus went on together, followed by the throng of people. The girl's family was already mourning her death, weeping and lamenting. Yeshua told them to stop, that the girl was only asleep. Someone actually laughed at Him." Joel's eyes rounded as he looked from Keziah to Zlata and back again. "Then He told the girl to rise, and she did so. Immediately."

"You saw her rise?" Keziah asked.

"No. I didn't, but I was outside when it happened. Yeshua took only a few of His disciples into the house. But we all heard everything about it later. Yeshua told the girl to rise, and then He told her mother to give her something to eat."

Keziah clucked her tongue. "Perhaps she wasn't really dead."

"She was dead."

"I wish I'd been there," Zlata said, more to herself than to the others.

Keziah grunted. "Taneli can't be pleased. He makes no secret how he feels about Yeshua. For Jairus to plead with Him for—" She broke off, ending instead with a shake of her head.

"You are right. Taneli was not pleased." Joel looked up at the sky, then rose from the stool. "I must go."

"Must you?" Heat rose in Zlata's cheeks as soon as the words escaped her.

But Joel seemed not to hear her. His attention was focused on Keziah, who was inviting him to share their evening meal when he completed the errand that had brought him to Bethsaida.

"It's kind of you, Keziah." He glanced at Zlata. "Are you sure you have enough?"

Once again, Keziah waved a hand in dismissal. "You are Taneli's trusted steward and Zlata's friend. Of course we have enough."

Joel pressed a hand to his chest and bowed slightly. "Then I thank you. I will break my return here and sup with you." He turned toward the road.

Zlata followed him as far as the stone fence. When it came time to say goodbye, she didn't know what to say, and so she remained silent, simply watching as his long strides carried him deeper into town. When he turned a street corner and disappeared from view, she made her way back to Keziah.

"That young man likes you," the older woman pronounced.

"He has been kind to me."

A frown furrowed Keziah's brow. "You are young. Why hasn't Taneli found you a husband in all these years?"

Emotions tightened Zlata's throat. She shook her head in answer.

"Ah. I see."

Did she see? Zlata wondered. Did she know Taneli blamed her for Yerik's death? That he didn't want her to have a life after she had deprived Yerik of his? Did she know Zlata blamed herself for all that had happened as well?

"We will pray, my daughter. We will pray for Adonai to change Taneli's heart."

A breeze off the Sea of Galilee helped cool the summer evening as Zlata set the stew and bread on the table, then joined Keziah and Joel to share in the supper.

It surprised her, how strange it felt to sit at table with a man. She'd served men, of course, as she'd done on the night of Simon's supper, but she hadn't sat down for a meal with a man since doing so with her husband more than eight years before. In Taneli's home, she either ate alone or with the female servants, and although Dara and the others were kind to her, she wasn't truly one of them. They knew she'd once been married to the master's son, which made her different from them.

But in Keziah's humble home, she'd found acceptance, and at this table, she was treated as an equal.

Perhaps some of the strangeness was also due to the way Joel looked at her. She'd recognized kindness in his eyes before. She'd recognized compassion too. But tonight, she thought she saw…affection. Was that possible? Could Keziah be right about him?

"That young man likes you."

Reaching to dip a chunk of bread into the vegetable stew, Zlata glanced in Joel's direction, pondering how Keziah's words—in combination with the look in Joel's eyes—made her feel. Again, it was odd and unfamiliar. No one had cared about her in so long. She had moved through days, weeks, months, and years in Taneli's household without anyone giving much notice, unless it was to give an order or a reprimand. Did she dare hope that someone might truly care? That she might have a life different from the one she had now?

"The stew is good," Joel said before popping a bite of stew-soaked bread into his mouth.

"Zlata made it." Keziah patted Zlata's shoulder. "She's made everything more comfortable for me since coming to stay."

Joel looked at Zlata. "Will you return to Capernaum soon?"

"In another week, I believe. Abra said I was to stay until Keziah is well."

"I wish she could be with me always, but alas, we do not always get what we want in life."

Zlata lowered her eyes again. *I wish I could stay too. I'm so much happier here.*

A thought niggled at her memory. Hadn't she felt happy on the day she arrived at Keziah's? Wasn't it because she believed her heart had been changed by her encounters with Yeshua? If that was true, if she had changed, then wouldn't her happiness last, even after she returned to the home of her in-laws?

"But I say to you, do not resist an evil person; but whoever slaps you on your right cheek, turn the other to him also."

Could she do as Yeshua instructed?

"But I say to you, love your enemies and pray for those who perse-cute you."

She had walked away when she heard Yeshua speak those words. Was she ready to obey them now?

"Zlata," Joel said softly, "you seem troubled."

She looked up again. "Do I?"

He nodded.

"I was…I was remembering something I heard Yeshua say. Something about loving my enemies."

He was silent a short while. Then he nodded. "I understand. I often have to stop and puzzle out His meanings. Often He ends a story with, 'If anyone has ears to hear, let him hear.' You remember, Zlata. He said it when He told the story of the sower that day by the lake. He commands His followers to comprehend, to listen, and to obey. I want to, but it may take me some time."

"He is a teacher of the law." Keziah leaned in. "Is it so different, what He says, than other teachers? Than the Pharisees? Different than Taneli?"

"Different? Yes." Joel closed his eyes. "Yeshua says, 'Beware of practicing your righteousness before men to be noticed by them; otherwise you have no reward with your Father who is in heaven. So when you give to the poor, do not sound a trumpet before you, as the hypocrites do in the synagogues and in the streets, so that they may be honored by men.'"

Zlata held her breath. In her ears, it seemed to be Yeshua's voice she heard instead of Joel's. And in her mind, it was Taneli she saw giving to the poor and loving the praise heaped upon him for doing so. She'd seen it happen many times but had never given thought to his actions before this. Did he understand that Yeshua meant someone like him?

She shivered. No wonder Taneli hated the teacher.

"I must go." Joel stood. "It will be near dark before I reach the vineyards."

Keziah looked up at him. "Come again. You are always welcome at my humble table."

"Thank you. Your kindness won't be forgotten." He turned toward Zlata, who had risen to her feet. "And yours."

The flutter in her chest kept her from smiling in response.

"We'll talk more about Yeshua when you return home."

"Yes," she whispered. "We'll talk more of Yeshua."

CHAPTER SIXTEEN

Keziah managed to keep Zlata with her in Bethsaida for several weeks beyond what was necessary. But Zlata's return to Capernaum could not be delayed forever. Eventually Abra sent for her. She gathered her few belongings and reluctantly said goodbye to the woman who had become her friend, and to the small one-room house that had seemed a sanctuary for much of the summer.

Dara greeted her when she stepped into the courtyard, obviously glad for another set of hands to help with the duties of the household. "The master has gone to Jerusalem on urgent business," the servant girl informed Zlata. "And the mistress is staying with her sister for several days."

Zlata took her traveling sack into the windowless storeroom that served as her bedchamber. Strange, how isolated it felt after living and sleeping in the room with Keziah for these past weeks. Although Keziah's sighs, grunts, and snores had kept her awake at first. Zlata had grown used to those sounds that had filled the nights.

Smiling at the memory, she left the room. There were chores awaiting her, but first she wanted to wash away the dust from her morning's journey. Weather permitting, she preferred to bathe in the stream that ran through Taneli's land.

There was a secluded place that she and other women fre-quented. But today she would make do with the private bath-ing facility in the courtyard.

Few houses in the region boasted such a luxury. Taneli was proud that his could, even though they didn't have a well or fountain in their courtyard as some larger homes did. Taneli's pride was probably why he allowed his servants to use the small bath area. Then they could talk about it in the marketplace or at the well or even in the synagogue. Strange that Zlata hadn't realized the reason before.

It was when Joel shared Yeshua's warning about practicing righteousness before men that Zlata had begun seeing Taneli in a new light. She had always assumed her father-in-law's adherence to the law was out of devotion to God. But perhaps that wasn't true. Perhaps it had more to do with his status before men.

She thought of her father, a hardworking fisherman, and Yerik, an equally hardworking vigneron. Men who worked with their hands, who knew the struggle of harvesting food from the earth and water. Men who loved God and trusted Him. They were men with simple but solid faith. It had been more than words by rote with them. Much more.

"Create in me a clean heart, O God, and renew a steadfast spirit within me."

Those were words she'd heard her father pray, and he'd trusted that the Lord would answer.

"Restore to me the joy of Your salvation and sustain me with a willing spirit."

Those were words she'd heard her husband pray, and he too had trusted that the Lord would answer.

Could she be like them? Could her faith become more real to her? Could she trust more?

Make my devotion to You real, Adonai. Let me practice living the way I should before You and not before men. Grant me a willing spirit.

As if in answer, she heard Yeshua's voice whisper in her heart, *"But I say to you, love your enemies and pray for those who persecute you."*

It wasn't only the Romans the Messiah asked her to love and pray for. It was Taneli as well. The second, she feared, would be more difficult for her than the first.

Joel came to the house in the early afternoon, asking to talk to Taneli, but when he learned both the master and mistress were away, he asked Dara if Zlata had by chance returned. When he learned she had, he asked to talk to her.

When Zlata stepped into the sunny courtyard a short while later, she was aware that others watched her, Dara from a doorway, a servant boy from the rooftop. For some reason that gave more import to the moment than it deserved. Would Taneli object to her talking to his steward? But how could he when he himself had sent her with messages to the man?

"It's nice to see you back," Joel said with a nod.

"Abra felt it was time for me to return. There is always much to do here."

"But I understand that she and the master are away from home at present."

"Yes."

A smile tweaked the corners of his mouth. "Then would it be possible for you to go with me? Yeshua is teaching in the hills, not far from here. We could sit and listen for as long as you feel able."

Yeshua. It had been many weeks since she had seen Him in the synagogue. She'd heard stories about Him, of course. Stories of teachings and healings and miracles. Some of them from Joel when he'd visited Bethsaida. But she longed to see and hear Him for herself once again. With both Abra and Taneli away, this was her best opportunity.

"And later," Joel continued, "you and I could discuss what we've heard."

She looked into his expressive eyes. He wanted to discuss what they heard with her. He wanted to learn her thoughts. The kindness made tears burn behind her eyes, and she turned away, saying, "Yes. I will go with you."

She went into the house.

"Dara, I'm going out for a while."

"With Joel?"

"He will accompany me. I am going to see Yeshua. He is teaching not far from here. Would you like to go with us?"

Dara's eyes grew wide as she shook her head. The girl knew what the master had told Zlata. Everyone in the household knew. They probably knew he had struck her for merely being in the wrong place at the wrong time, for chancing upon Him and pausing to observe.

"You should come with us. Yeshua is…He is different than you might think."

The servant shook her head again, more vigorously this time.

"You will not tell anyone where I've gone? Taneli said I was not to follow the rabbi. He didn't say I couldn't listen from afar."

"I won't tell, but I don't think you should go."

Despite the anxiety that coiled in her belly, Zlata ignored the warning. "Thank you, Dara." She reached out and squeezed the girl's hand. "Thank you for being my friend."

Dara's eyes widened. It made Zlata wonder how much more she might have done through the years. Maybe feeling that she didn't fit in with others who worked for Taneli had more to do with her own actions than theirs.

After adjusting her headscarf, she returned to the courtyard and followed Joel toward the main road leading out of Capernaum. It wasn't long before they were part of a stream of people. Like Joel, they had learned where the teacher was that day and wanted to see and hear Him. There were people Zlata recognized, but there were many she'd never seen before. Perhaps they were strangers to Capernaum who had journeyed long distances for a chance to see the teacher. She saw a man with a twisted leg, a crutch under one arm, struggling to keep up. She saw a blind woman being led by the hand. She saw excitement on the faces of many, desperation on the faces of others.

When they arrived at the hillside, people crowded in as close to Yeshua as was possible. Some moved above Him. Most stayed below, hoping His voice would carry to them.

As she and Joel were finding a place to sit on the ground, Zlata saw Bilhah and Hevel. The sight of them together, both healed in their own way by the rabbi, warmed her heart. Bilhah, wearing a dark brown headscarf, turned her head at that moment. The peace Zlata could see in her old friend's eyes stole her breath away. Bilhah smiled and waved, then motioned to an open spot near her. Zlata moved to fill it, Joel right behind. No one spoke a greeting, instead turning their attention to Yeshua.

He spoke in a voice that seemed both gentle and strong at the same time. It held a mixture of love and authority.

"For this reason I say to you, do not worry about your life, as to what you will eat; nor for your body, as to what you will put on. For life is more than food, and the body more than cloth-ing." His gaze moved slowly over the people who surrounded Him. "Consider the ravens, for they neither sow nor reap; they have no storeroom nor barn, and yet God feeds them; how much more valuable you are than the birds!" His eyes met with Zlata's, and for a breath, He seemed to see only her. "And which of you by worrying can add a single hour to his life's span? If then you cannot do even a very little thing, why do you worry about other matters?"

You are the Messiah.

She'd heard Taneli and his friends curse the notion that Yeshua could be the Messiah. Despite the miracles taking place all around the Sea of Galilee, wherever Yeshua went, they said it couldn't be so. But she was seated near a man who'd been mute and could now speak. She was seated beside a woman whose life had been marred by sin and now was made clean. But miracles weren't enough for Taneli.

You are *the Messiah,* her heart sang, *and I have lived to see You come to the people of Israel.*

"Do not be afraid, little flock, for your Father has chosen gladly to give you the kingdom."

Help me, Adonai, not to be afraid. Help me not to worry about all those other matters.

CHAPTER SEVENTEEN

For Zlata, the following weeks passed in a golden haze. As often as possible, she and Joel met in private to talk about what they had heard Yeshua teach, trying to find the deeper meaning in His words, trying to ascertain how His teachings meant they should live each day. Their shared belief in the rabbi had bonded them, and it was a secret Zlata held close in her spirit.

She wasn't in love with Joel. That was something she didn't want to feel for any man ever again. But because of Yeshua the deep bitterness that had turned her heart to stone had diminished over the summer, leaving her strangely contented for the first time since the death of her husband. Not completely happy but content. Peaceful.

After Taneli's return from Jerusalem, her father-in-law seethed and stormed about the teacher from Nazareth even more than before. He and Nathan were often part of the crowd that followed Yeshua, although for very different reasons than most who sought Him out. Many wanted to hear the teacher speak because they believed He held answers. Others were ill and searching for physical healing. But Taneli wanted to find a way to destroy the man who talked about the kingdom of God with such authority, a man who had dared to refer to the Pharisees and scribes as hypocrites and robbers and to Himself as the Son of Man.

Sometimes, as Zlata worked in the house or in the courtyard, she would overhear Taneli as he ranted on about something Yeshua had said. Taneli didn't mean to share the teacher's words with her, of course, but that's what he did. And Zlata listened with care, accepting what she heard as gifts for her soul. She collected them, repeated them, memorized them.

"The eye is the lamp of your body; when your eye is clear, your whole body also is full of light...."

"For you pay tithe of mint and rue and every kind of garden herb, and yet disregard justice and the love of God...."

"You too, be ready; for the Son of Man is coming at an hour that you do not expect...."

"I tell you that in the same way, there will be more joy in heaven over one sinner who repents than over ninety-nine righteous persons who need no repentance...."

"Blessed is he who does not take offense at Me...."

"So take care how you listen...."

"Strive to enter through the narrow door; for many, I tell you, will seek to enter and will not be able...."

"For whoever is ashamed of Me and My words, the Son of Man will be ashamed of him when He comes in His glory...."

As farmers harvested their crops that fall, Zlata began to pray to her heavenly Father. It was a new prayer, a prayer Yeshua had taught His disciples and then Bilhah, in secret, had passed along to Zlata. Without consciously making it happen, she found herself thinking of her father-in-law every time she whispered the words about forgiving her debtors during her morning prayer. She understood what God wanted her to do. But how could she do it?

Taneli never forgave anyone anything. It wasn't in him. Bilhah was an example of that. Even four months after Simon's supper, he still brought up "that woman" who'd interrupted the proceedings, condemning her, outraged that Yeshua had said she was forgiven for her sins. It didn't matter to Taneli that Bilhah had put her old ways behind her, that she'd found a place to live and respectable employment, that she was a different person today. Taneli's judgment remained unchanged. It was another reason why Zlata was just as cautious and secretive about seeing her childhood friend as she was about her moments with Joel.

As winter approached, more strangers from near and far poured into Capernaum in hopes of seeing Yeshua. They slept in the open, making their campsites wherever space remained. They crowded the town and the surrounding countryside. The numbers ebbed whenever Yeshua traveled elsewhere, then flowed back in when He returned. Merchants appreciated the trade that the influx of people brought them, but Capernaum also suffered an increase in beggars and thieves, and more unrest than before.

Another reason for Taneli to rage against the rabbi. One night he decided that Abra and Zlata would not leave the house unless they were with him. The female servants would fetch water and go to the marketplace, but Abra and Zlata would remain within the confines of the house.

Zlata's world suddenly became even smaller than before and stayed that way far longer than she expected.

PART II

Spring, during the third year of Yeshua's Galilean ministry

Jesus was going through all the cities and villages, teaching in their synagogues and proclaiming the gospel of the kingdom, and healing every kind of disease and every kind of sickness. Seeing the people, He felt compassion for them, because they were distressed and dispirited like sheep without a shepherd. Then He said to His disciples, "The harvest is plentiful, but the workers are few. Therefore beseech the Lord of the harvest to send out workers into His harvest."

—Matthew 9:35–38, NASB

And He called the twelve together, and gave them power and authority over all the demons and to heal diseases. And He sent them out to proclaim the kingdom of God and to perform healing.

—Luke 9:1–2, NASB

CHAPTER EIGHTEEN

A strong spring wind blew off the lake that early morning as Zlata made her way to the well. After five miserable months, she didn't know what made Taneli relax his ruling regarding his wife and daughter-in-law. Perhaps he noticed the household didn't run as well as it used to. Perhaps he didn't always have the fish he wanted or the meat he wanted or the vegetables and fruit he wanted because Zlata hadn't done the shopping in the marketplace. Or perhaps he was tired of Abra's complaints about feeling like a prisoner in her own home.

Whatever the reason, Zlata was outside today, completely alone, and she breathed in the cool air of freedom like someone surfacing from a long time under water.

Adonai, if I could see Bilhah or Joel, the morning would be perfect.

Over the winter, she'd caught the occasional glimpse of Joel when he'd come to see the master on matters related to the vineyard. But never had she had the opportunity to talk to him. She missed their discussions about Yeshua. She missed exploring the meaning of the rabbi's words. While she still caught snippets of Yeshua's teachings from Taneli, it wasn't the same thing as hearing it for herself or talking about it with someone who didn't despise the teacher.

The wind caught her headscarf and sent one end of it flapping behind her. She stopped long enough to catch it and wrap it in place again.

Many women were at the well when Zlata arrived, a number of strangers among them. A few who were familiar asked Zlata why they hadn't seen her for such a long while. Had she been ill? Had she been away? No, she hadn't been ill. No, she hadn't been away. That was all she could answer as she looked all around, still hoping to see Bilhah. But that prayer went unanswered. At last, feeling she had lingered as long as possible, she started the walk back to the house, the water jug balanced on her shoulder.

She was halfway to her destination when she saw a cart with a missing wheel on the side of the road. A donkey had been unhitched, and it grazed nearby. A small boy struggled to set the heavy wheel back in place while a man lifted the cart off the ground, bracing it with his back. Zlata might have walked by without more than a glance in their direction, but then she saw a woman who sat with her back against a tree, a child of about a year old cradled in her arms, her face hidden by her headscarf.

"Was anyone hurt?" Zlata asked as she stopped, then moved closer.

The woman looked up. She appeared to be about Zlata's own age, pretty with large dark eyes. Tears streaked her dust-covered cheeks.

"Are you all right?" Zlata set the water jar on the ground.

"I'm fine," the woman answered in a whispery voice, her gaze lowering again to the child in her arms. "But our daughter. She's not well."

"How can I help?"

The woman looked at the large jar. "Could you spare some water?"

"Of course."

The woman produced a cup from a cloth bag beside her, and Zlata filled it from the jar then watched as the worried mother placed the cup to her daughter's lips, coaxing the child to drink.

"My name is Zlata."

"I'm Miriam," the woman answered without looking up.

"Where is your home?" Her gaze moved to the two-wheeled cart.

"In Emmaus."

"Emmaus?" So many days of rough travel in that miserable little cart. It couldn't have been easy. Especially with a sick child.

"My husband and I are seeking the rabbi named Yeshua."

The explanation didn't surprise Zlata. Wasn't that what drew most people to Galilee these days?

"The physicians say there is nothing to be done for Orpah. Yeshua is our only remaining hope."

Zlata nodded. She would have traveled to Egypt and beyond if it would have saved Uriah's life. If only Yeshua had been in Capernaum all those years ago, perhaps her son would be walking by her side even now.

"Do you know where we can find the rabbi?"

"I'm sorry. I don't know. Yeshua travels about the countryside. Sometimes He teaches by the lake." She pointed. "Sometimes in the hills. Sometimes in towns across the water."

Tears welled in Miriam's eyes.

"I'm sure someone in Capernaum will know where He can be found." She didn't add that Yeshua was often away for several weeks at a time.

Softly, Miriam asked, "What if we're too late?"

"I may know someone who can help you. When you enter the town, ask for the shop of Jonah the weaver. There is a woman who works for him. Her name is Bilhah. Perhaps she will know where you can find the teacher today."

"Thank you." Miriam reached out and grasped Zlata's hand. "Thank you."

A lump formed in Zlata's throat, making it impossible to answer. All she could do was nod.

"Miriam," her husband called. "We are ready."

Zlata stood and picked up her water jar. "I wish you well."

She set off down the road, then stopped and looked back, watching as Miriam's husband helped her into the back of the cart, their daughter still cradled close to her breast.

Have mercy, Father. Put this family in Yeshua's path. Give them the healing they seek.

The cart jerked into motion, heading in the opposite direction. Zlata turned and hurried on toward Taneli's house.

Early that same afternoon, Zlata was working in the household garden when she heard the sound of the courtyard door opening. She glanced up, expecting it to be one of the servants.

Instead, she saw Keziah step into the courtyard. Joy leapt in her heart at the sight of the woman.

"Keziah!" She rose swiftly, brushing at the dirt on her tunic.

"Greetings, Zlata. You look well."

"And you. Is Abra expecting you? She didn't tell anyone we were to have a guest."

Keziah shook her head. "I am not expected, but I hope my cousin will be happy to see me."

"Of course she will be happy. Come. Sit down and rest. I'll let her know you're here. Then I'll bring water so you can wash away the dust from your travels. The day is warm, and you've had a long walk."

Keziah sat on a stool in the shade, releasing a grateful sigh as she did so.

Before Zlata could move toward the main entrance, Abra came out of the house. "Cousin. How good to see you. But what brings you to Capernaum?"

With a nod in Keziah's direction, Zlata went to fetch the water for washing. By the time she returned, the two women were deep in conversation. Without interrupting them, Zlata knelt to wash Keziah's feet. A short while later, she made her way back to the garden. Her attention soon wandered as the two older women visited about family members, the price of pottery and linen, and local gossip.

It seemed a long while later when Keziah asked something about Yeshua. At the mention of His name, Zlata's attention focused once again, and she raised her eyes.

"Do not speak of Him in this house," Abra said sternly. "Do not mention Him while you are here. Taneli does not allow it."

Zlata almost snorted. Taneli didn't allow *others* to talk of the rabbi. But it seemed that he talked of little else when he was at home.

"But the teacher is spoken of everywhere," Keziah said. "Have you not heard what happened near Bethsaida just last week?"

Zlata expected Abra to silence her cousin again. But after a quick glance toward the courtyard door—as if she feared the imminent return of her husband—she said, "No. What happened?"

"Many people followed Him there, as they seem to do everywhere. Thousands of them. They were not in Bethsaida, of course. They were in the countryside nearby. A quite desolate area too. They say there were five thousand men. Many women and children too. Crowding in. Trying to hear Him speak. Hoping for a healing."

"Five thousand men?" Abra asked the question on a hushed breath.

"Five thousand."

"Were you there? Did you go to see Him yourself?"

Keziah shook her head. "No. I wasn't there. But I wish I had been. I wish these old bones of mine were up to hiking through the hills, but they aren't."

Abra grunted.

"After many hours, Yeshua's men told Him to send the people away because they were hungry and needed to find food and lodging. Instead, He told His disciples to feed the people. It's said all they had between them were five loaves and two fish."

Abra pulled back. "That wouldn't feed this household. Let alone so many."

"I know."

Zlata's heart thrummed with anticipation as she listened.

"What happened next?" Abra asked. "Did the people leave on their own?"

"No. Yeshua had His men seat them in groups of fifty. Then He took the loaves and fish, blessed the food, broke it into pieces, and gave it to His disciples to set before the people."

Abra scoffed. "That wouldn't take long."

Keziah's face broke into a smile. "But you're wrong. He kept giving the pieces of bread and fish and giving it and giving it until everyone was fed." She lifted her hands, as if in triumph. "And when they picked up what was left over, there were twelve baskets full remaining."

Zlata saw Abra's head start to turn toward her and quickly looked down, moving her hands over the soil. *Please don't let her guess I was listening.* She slid her knees slightly to the right, her gaze locked on the ground.

Abra said, "It's an impossible story. Taneli says Yeshua pays people to spread such lies."

"Where did all that food come from then?" Keziah insisted.

"I don't know. But they must have paid numerous merchants. Paid them enough that they wouldn't tell the truth, no matter who asked."

"Yeshua isn't a wealthy man. He's an itinerate teacher. He couldn't afford such a bribe."

"Then His men paid."

Keziah huffed her disbelief. "His disciples are common men too. Fishermen, some of them, from right here in Capernaum and Bethsaida. You may know some of them from the synagogue. You may know their families."

Zlata dared to look up again. Even from the side, Abra's scowl was evident.

Keziah crossed her arms over her chest. "Some say He is Elijah or one of the prophets come back to life."

"And those who say it are fools."

"Others say He is surely the Messiah. For without the blessing of God, He could not do the miracles He has done."

Abra stood. "Keziah, you are my blood. But if you continue to speak of such things, you will have to leave. Do you hear me? You will not be welcome here if you tell such fabrications again." She walked toward the doorway into the house.

Keziah's gaze moved to Zlata, and in that moment, Zlata knew the story had been told for her benefit, not Abra's. She smiled her gratitude before turning her attention once more to the garden.

CHAPTER NINETEEN

It seemed to Zlata, as she and Keziah were jostled about in the marketplace the following morning, that the entire five thousand men and their families who'd been in the Bethsaida hills had made their way to Capernaum over the past week. And they were all hungry and needing to be fed once again. And this time the Messiah wasn't present to multiply loaves and fishes. This time they needed to buy their food and other supplies from the various venders.

No wonder Taneli complained so much about the crowds. Even as glad as Zlata was that her father-in-law had loosened his restrictions, she felt anxiety being surrounded by so many, her body jabbed by elbows, her ears assaulted by shouts, myriad conversations, and the bleats and squawks of animals. Worse still, the increased population seemed to concern the Romans. It seemed soldiers were everywhere.

With great effort and some good fortune, she managed to purchase the items she'd been sent into town to buy. If only she and Keziah didn't have to fight their way back through the crowd in order to return to the house. Perhaps it would be better to go the opposite direction and then make their way back on a road that skirted Capernaum on the north side. She was about to suggest as much to Keziah when a firm hand grasped her arm above the elbow. A startled gasp escaped her throat.

"Zlata. Keziah. Come with me."

Relief replaced her alarm at the sound of Joel's voice, and she allowed him to draw her into a narrow street, away from the bustling marketplace, Keziah following close behind.

When they stopped at last, Zlata said, "I didn't expect it to be this bad."

"I'm glad I saw you. You shouldn't come to town when it's like this. Not alone."

"She isn't alone," Keziah said, leveling her shoulders. "I'm with her."

Joel looked at the older woman, then back to Zlata. "I meant both of you. There was a fight in the marketplace last night. People were hurt."

"I wanted to come. I've been kept shut away far too long." A shudder passed through her, hating the idea that she might be denied freedom for a second time.

Understanding filled Joel's eyes. "It's good to see you. I've missed our talks."

"I've missed them too."

"I must get you home. This way."

Zlata didn't need Joel to lead her through the back streets. She'd grown up in Capernaum. She'd known these streets all her life. Still, she found it comforting to follow him, to stare at his broad shoulders, to feel protected by someone strong and sure.

Joel slowed his steps when they were beyond the close cluster of houses. "I'll take you back this way." He motioned toward the northern road, obviously having the same idea that she'd considered earlier. "I was told Yeshua is walking today to the south. The news will spread, and the people will soon follow Him there."

"There are so many more of them than there used to be." From the rooftop of the house, Zlata had seen people coming and going along the road for all of the months of her captivity, but she hadn't truly perceived the increase.

"Yeshua's fame has grown." Joel shook his head, his expression grave. "I fear for Him. People flock to Galilee from far beyond Jerusalem. The Romans don't like how the crowds follow Him about, even here. The Pharisees and Sadducees hate Him for what He teaches—and for what He says about them. Many of His followers think He should leave the region, go where others can't find Him, stop teaching for a time. The mood feels…precarious."

"Leave?" Zlata whispered. The thought made her heart sink. What if she never had the chance to hear Yeshua teach again? What if she never fully understood the meaning of His words? What if—

"Zlata!"

She turned to see who had called her name. It was the cart and donkey she saw first. Then she saw Miriam hurrying toward her from a nearby grove of trees. The smile Miriam wore told Zlata everything, even before her gaze shifted to the child in Miriam's arms. A child who was awake and bright-eyed and full of health, so unlike the one who'd been nestled in her desperate mother's arms the previous morning.

"We found Him, Zlata. Yeshua healed her. We were able to press through the crowd to reach Him, and He healed her. Orpah is well."

"I can see." Zlata reached out and touched the child's cheek. Her heart swelled with joy.

"He healed others too. We saw it happen. Many others. He made the lame walk and the blind to see. There were lepers He made clean."

For an instant, a familiar bitterness twisted inside of Zlata. She wanted to say she was glad for Miriam. No, not just say it. She *was* glad. And yet she wondered: Why this woman's child and not her own? Couldn't Adonai have shown mercy to Uriah? Was it her son's fault he'd been born long before Yeshua of Nazareth came to Capernaum?

But then she remembered the night of Simon's supper, remembered the moment when Yeshua had raised His eyes and looked at her standing in the shadows, remembered the feeling that had taken root in her heart. She wasn't the same woman she'd been before that, and she didn't want to go back to being her.

"I am happy for you, Miriam," she said, focusing her attention once again on the young mother. "Will you stay in Capernaum? Will you go to hear Yeshua teach again?"

"No." Miriam shook her head. "We start back to Emmaus today. My husband must return to his work."

"May God bless your journey and keep you safe."

"Thank you. I won't forget your kindness yesterday. I won't ever forget." Miriam's gaze flicked beyond Zlata's shoulder to where Joel and Keziah stood. But then she turned and hurried back to her husband and son.

"The child was sick?" Keziah asked, stepping to Zlata's right side.

"She was dying. I saw her only yesterday. The mother was desperate, and her only hope was Yeshua."

"The child is well now, God be praised."

"Yes." She spoke the word softly, watching the small family ready for its trip south.

"And such things you have seen with your own eyes," Keziah said, a sound of wonder in her voice.

"Yes." Zlata smiled. "Yes, I have seen such things with my own eyes."

"They were only stories to me until now. Not people. Only stories."

Zlata put an arm around Keziah's shoulders and squeezed her close. Then, with Joel taking the lead, the three of them continued on their way.

CHAPTER TWENTY

"At last!" Taneli exclaimed. "If He is wise, He will stay in Phoenicia and never come back. And may the rabble stay there with Him."

From her workplace on the rooftop, Zlata set aside her sewing and went to look down into the courtyard. Nathan and Simon had both come to call on Taneli. The three men were seated in the shade, for the moment Taneli wearing one of his rare smiles.

Heart sinking, Zlata turned away from the ledge. Over the past week, she had hoped to find an opportunity to hear Yeshua teach again. Now it seemed there wouldn't be. Yeshua had left Capernaum and gone north, as He'd been encouraged to do by some of His own disciples. Or so Joel had told her.

What if the teacher didn't return? That's what her father-in-law hoped. What if He found the region of Tyre more welcoming than Galilee? Or at least safer?

She sank onto the cushion and leaned her back against the stone and mortar wall. Closing her eyes, she pictured Yeshua as He sat on the hillside, gesturing with His hands, sweeping the crowd with His gaze. She remembered Him in the synagogue as He read from the scriptures, His voice strong. She recalled the night of Simon's supper as He'd reclined at the table, dipping His food into the same bowl as the man who wanted to be rid of Him. She wanted more encounters to remember. Many more. Now more opportunities seemed doubtful.

Drawing and releasing a deep breath, she reminded herself how blessed she was. Taneli had wanted to keep her completely away from the teacher. Yet over the past year, Zlata had observed Yeshua half a dozen times. She'd heard Him speak with her own ears. She'd seen Him heal Hevel with her own eyes. She knew He'd restored Miriam's daughter. Thousands of others had traveled to Galilee. Perhaps they had seen the rabbi. Perhaps they hadn't. But Zlata lived in Capernaum, Yeshua's chosen residence, and God had given her glimpses of Him to be remembered and treasured. She would hold them tightly and keep hoping she might add to them.

The voices of the men carried to her again. They were arguing about something. A fine point from the law, from what she could tell. That wasn't unusual. Men like Taneli could talk and argue for hours over the meaning of just a few words. It was their life. Most often, when she took the time to listen to them, she couldn't understand anything. It made her feel ignorant.

Why didn't she feel that same way when she listened to Yeshua? Like the men in the courtyard below, the rabbi had said many things she didn't understand. Yet all it did was create a burning in her chest to try harder, to listen closer, to seek answers. Never did she feel unintelligent.

She took up her sewing, wishing at the same time that Keziah hadn't returned to Bethsaida already. It would have been good to have her company while she worked, to feel free to share her thoughts about Yeshua.

And Joel. She wished she could share her thoughts with Joel. She hadn't seen him since the day he'd escorted her and Keziah out of the crowded marketplace and home again.

She frowned. Joel was a good friend to her, and he was often in her thoughts. But did he want to be more than a friend? She wasn't sure. Sometimes she thought so. Other times she didn't. Years before, Abra had made it clear that Taneli had no intention of finding Zlata another husband. They had given her shelter after the deaths of her husband and child. Her place was to serve them, to be thankful they hadn't cast her out with nothing, as they could have.

But what if a man like Joel were to approach Taneli and ask for her in marriage? Would Taneli agree to such a thing? Joel was not a man of means. He wouldn't have a bride price. Not one that would impress her father-in-law, at any rate. He worked for Taneli. His simple home was provided by Taneli.

Would I wish to marry Joel if he wanted me?

She shook her head in answer to the silent question. It wasn't wise to contemplate such a matter. Her father had chosen well for her because he'd loved her and wanted her to be happy. If Taneli chose a husband for her, he would do so for very different reasons, certainly not because he loved her, and he wouldn't care whether or not she was happy. Better he not think of her at all. Or at the very least, better he think it a punishment for her to remain an unmarried servant in his household.

That afternoon, Zlata and Dara went to the stream that flowed through Taneli's land on its way to the lake. Abra wanted them to weave a few new baskets for the household, and they needed boughs that were young, green, and pliable. Zlata's favorite branches for basketmaking came from the willow trees, and she knew just where to find them.

But when they reached the stream, Zlata chose to sit on the bank, remove her sandals, and put her feet in the water. A sigh of pleasure escaped her.

"It's warm today," Dara said as she mimicked Zlata's actions.

"Mmm." Zlata closed her eyes and turned her face toward the sun.

"The road is not as crowded today. There were fewer strangers at the well this morning."

"I heard Taneli say that Yeshua has gone to Tyre, and the people have followed Him there or gone home." She looked at the girl seated next to her. "I still hope to see Him again."

Dara dipped her hands into the cool stream. "I never saw Him. All this time He was in Capernaum, and I never saw Him. Not even once."

"Are you sorry for that?"

Dara shook her head, nodded, then shook her head again.

Zlata gave her a small smile. "He may return. I pray that He'll return. I want to listen to Him teach. His words…" She let her voice trail into silence.

"The master would be furious if he knew that's what you want." Dara's gaze flicked to Zlata's cheek, as if she could still see the red mark from the time Taneli backhanded her.

Almost a year had passed since that day, but the moment was clear in Zlata's mind. And apparently just as clear in Dara's.

The servant tipped her head to one side and gave Zlata a long look. "You've changed."

"Have I?" she asked, even though she knew it was true.

"You aren't as unhappy as you used to be."

Zlata nodded.

"What changed you?"

She was silent a few moments before answering, "Yeshua."

"How?"

"I'm not sure. I only know He has."

"But you are still afraid."

"Afraid?"

"Of the master."

Zlata wanted to deny it, but she couldn't. She *was* afraid of Taneli. How could she not be? He had all the power. She was only a woman, a widow with no family, no possessions, no money. He had the right to turn her out for any reason. Or for no reason at all.

"I hope he never finds out about you and Joel."

Zlata's breath caught. "What are you saying? Nothing improper has happened between us. Joel is a friend. Nothing more."

Dara's eyes said she had her doubts.

"We are friends," Zlata insisted again. "That is all. And we…we both want to learn all that Yeshua teaches."

"You would be in even more trouble with the master for that."

I know. And I'm afraid. But I can't stop believing He is…the One.

Dara stood, the water running around her ankles. "I'll start with those over there." She made her way across the stream and began cutting off supple branches with a knife, placing them in a pile on the ground.

Zlata watched the servant girl for a time, but her thoughts were elsewhere. Confusion mingled with the fear Dara's comments had brought to the surface. In most ways, she was invisible to her father-in-law and preferred to keep it that way. There were many good reasons why. But when it came to Yeshua, she had dared to defy Taneli. She'd done so carefully, but it was still defiance. Defiance for which he would punish her severely were he to learn of it.

"As we forgive our debtors."

She hadn't forgiven Taneli. Not for the way he'd treated her since Yerik's death. Not for the coldness she lived with still. Not for the time he'd struck her. She feared him and she hadn't forgiven him.

I don't know how to forgive him.

She pushed herself up from the bank and began to collect branches for the baskets. Anything to drive away the thoughts that troubled her.

CHAPTER TWENTY-ONE

With Yeshua teaching elsewhere, life in Capernaum settled into an old, familiar pattern. While people continued to seek the rabbi, there weren't as many as before, and they
passed through the town on the northern shore of the Sea of
Galilee rather than staying for days, even weeks at a time.

"His popularity may have waned here," Taneli stated to his
wife one night, "but still He is a danger to us all. He continues
to teach and influence those who wish to be fooled. Why hasn't
someone been able to stop Him? I don't understand. We try
but we fail. He frustrates us at every turn."

As Zlata made her way to the marketplace the morning after
she'd overheard Taneli's latest complaint, she prayed that Yeshua
would continue to confound and confuse men like her father-in-
law. She prayed that He would remain safe, wherever He was.

When her basket contained the wheat, barley, and fruit
she'd been sent to buy, she made her way along the narrow,
winding streets to the shop of Jonah the weaver. Bilhah sat at
the loom, working yarn through the frame.

"Good morning, Zlata," Jonah greeted her as she stepped
through the doorway.

Jonah was a tall, broad-shouldered man with a scarred
face. Some people were frightened of him because of his size

and the injury he'd suffered in a fire as a child, but he didn't frighten Zlata. She knew him to be a gentle giant with a good heart.

Bilhah glanced up from the loom. "My friend!" Smiling, she rose and hurried forward.

Zlata set her basket on the floor, and the two women clasped hands. "You are well?" she asked her friend.

"I am well. And you?"

Zlata nodded.

"I haven't seen you in so long." Bilhah squeezed Zlata's fingers before releasing her hands.

"Many months."

"Joel told me the rules that were imposed in the household." Bilhah drew Zlata toward the loom and soon they were both seated on wooden stools. "I was sorry for you. I missed the times we were able to talk."

Zlata lowered her voice to a near whisper. "You have followed the rabbi? You have heard Him teach since we last spoke?"

"Yes. When He is near Capernaum, I often go to listen and to see what He does." She glanced at her employer. "Jonah has been generous to allow it."

"I'm glad." Zlata drew a quick breath. "Will Yeshua return to the region, do you think?"

A shadow passed over Bilhah's face. "Yes, but it feels as if the time for Him to be here grows short."

"What do you mean?"

"I'm not sure. It is simply a feeling I have." Bilhah shook her head slowly. "His words are not always easy to understand. Most rabbis teach with parables at times, and one must seek for the truth within the stories. Yeshua's parables are no different. Many aren't willing to look for the deeper meaning, but I try. And often, what He says goes against what I have thought was true." She glanced across the shop. "Talking with Jonah often helps me find the answers."

Zlata's gaze followed Bilhah's. Jonah stood at a worktable, a frown of concentration knitting his thick eyebrows. She thought of Joel. Of his frequent smiles and his boisterous laughter. Of how seriously he listened and then dissected the teachings of Yeshua. Of his eagerness to understand and obey.

Strange, wasn't it? The way the rabbi had brought Bilhah and Zlata together, first with each other and later with men they might not ever have known beyond a word of greeting and certainly never to have befriended.

"Remember," Bilhah said, "how Yeshua looked at me on the night He first saw me?"

The question drew Zlata's attention back to her friend.

"He looks upon everyone that same way. With compassion. With mercy. And He treats women with the same respect that He offers men. I have never known another like Him. No one has. Because of it, there are a number of women who provide support so He can go on teaching and ministering to those in need. They are counted among His disciples."

Zlata had heard, of course, of the women who traveled with Yeshua and His disciples, helping to care for their needs, preparing food, fetching water. These weren't ordinary camp followers to be looked down upon in disgust—although Taneli thought otherwise. Some were women of means, others who gave generously from whatever they had. Some had been physically healed, including one who'd been delivered of seven evil spirits. Another was married to a man in power in Herod's own household. What must it be like to be one of those women, to be that near to Yeshua on a daily basis? To hear Him speak while eating supper by the fire with only His closest associates around. To follow after Him as He traveled a dusty road, going from village to village. To witness one miracle, one healing, after another. To be taught, day in and day out, by the Messiah Himself. Imagining it took her breath away.

As if reading Zlata's thoughts, Bilhah said, "If I could, I would be one of them. I would follow and support Him too. Wouldn't you, if you were free to do so?"

Zlata could almost hear her father-in-law raging. She knew his determination to destroy Yeshua. He wanted to devastate the rabbi's followers as well, the ones he called sinners and prostitutes, tax collectors and beggars, liars and thieves. A shudder passed through her as she imagined Taneli finding her among them. He would want to kill her rather than allow such a thing to happen.

Not wanting to admit her own cowardice, she chose not to answer Bilhah.

Her friend glanced at the loom. "I must finish this," she said, an apology in her voice.

"It's all right." Zlata rose. "It is time I returned to the house. I only had a few things to purchase in the marketplace, and it is not so crowded now."

Bilhah reached out to touch her hand. "Be of good courage, my friend."

Zlata nodded and left the weaver's shop.

As she walked along the streets, back toward the market and the town gates, Zlata's thoughts remained on what Bilhah had said. About how she wished she could follow Yeshua. About how she wanted to serve Him and be one of His disciples. Zlata envied her friend, that she had the courage to even consider such a possibility.

With her eyes on the ground and her thoughts elsewhere, she turned a corner and bumped into a hard form.

"Hey, there. Watch where you're going."

The harsh voice drew Zlata's gaze upward. A Roman soldier, with his helmet, red cape, and sword—all symbols of terror to Zlata—glared at her.

She shrank back from him. "I...I am sorry, my lord. I didn't...I didn't mean—"

"You Jews never mean to do anything." He continued to scowl at her for what seemed a very long time. Then a half smile lifted one corner of his mouth. "But they aren't all as pretty as you, so I suppose I can overlook it this time."

Quivering now, Zlata dipped her head so that she was looking at the man's sandals. Hastily, she tugged her headscarf forward.

The soldier grunted. "Be off with you. And pay attention to where you're walking."

Not waiting for a second command, she scurried around him, heart racing. She didn't slow her pace until she was far beyond the gates of Capernaum. About halfway to Taneli's house, she found she was shaking so hard her legs would no longer hold her upright. She left the road and sank into the long grass beneath a tree. It felt as if her lungs were starved for air, but she couldn't seem to draw in enough to satisfy.

Closing her eyes and hugging herself, she tried to still the trembling by sheer force of will. It didn't work.

But then it came to her, a memory from childhood, when she'd been no more than eight or nine. She'd been awakened by a nightmare, and her father had come to sit beside her. He'd dried her tears and asked, "What do we do when we're afraid, Zlata?"

"We remember Adonai."

"And what does Adonai tell us?"

Obediently, she had recited the words written by the prophet Isaiah. "Do not fear, for I am with you; do not anxiously look about you, for I am your God. I will strengthen you, surely I will help you, surely I will uphold you with My righteous right hand."

Her father had nodded and kissed her forehead. "Adonai is always with you, Zlata. He is your God. He will uphold you with His righteous right hand. Never forget it."

Zlata's trembling lessened at the memory.

And then another memory came to her from a year ago. Yeshua looking at the crowd of people all around, saying, "Are not two sparrows sold for a cent? And yet not one of them will fall to the ground apart from your Father. But the very hairs of your head are all numbered. So do not fear; you are more valuable than many sparrows."

"Do not fear."

The shivering and shaking ceased at last, and she drew a deep breath.

"What do I do when I'm afraid?" she whispered, looking up at the sky through the limbs of the tree. "I have remembered Adonai." She drew another breath. "And I'll remember Yeshua too."

CHAPTER TWENTY-TWO

A few weeks later, Taneli and his friends departed Capernaum for the north. News had been brought to them from Phoenicia that had brought the rage back into Taneli's face. He didn't speak of the details, although it was obvious it had to do with Yeshua. His anger was always tied to the teacher these days.

Zlata wasn't sorry to see Taneli leave. Nobody was when he was in such a mood.

On the next Sabbath, while Abra napped and the other servants rested from their duties, Zlata slipped away to sit by the lake. The day had grown warm, but there was a pleasant breeze bringing cooler air off the water. A number of boats had been pulled halfway onto the shore. Like the owners, the boats also rested on this day.

Zlata made certain she sat in a place obscured from the road. With travel for Jews restricted on the Sabbath, she wasn't likely to be seen by many of her own people, but the Romans didn't take this seventh day off. While soldiers didn't seem to patrol this main thoroughfare as frequently now that Yeshua was teaching elsewhere, her encounter with the Roman in Capernaum on the day she'd visited the weaver's shop had made her extra cautious.

Remembering it now made her shiver.

"So do not fear," she whispered. "I am more valuable than many sparrows."

Laughter from down the lakeshore drew her gaze. A couple walked beside the lapping water, holding hands. As they drew closer, she saw that it was Zebedee and Salome. A short while later, they noticed her. Smiling, they approached.

"Zlata," Salome said, "I see you seek the cooler air too."

"Yes."

Salome touched her husband's chest with the flat of one hand. "It is hard to keep Zebedee away from the lake, even on the Sabbath."

"My father was the same."

Zebedee sat on a large rock while Salome settled on the bank near Zlata.

Salome released a soft sigh. "We thought our sons would rather be on the water. They grew up there. They learned to be fishermen by observing their father and loved it. But now…" She sighed again, but it wasn't a sad sound. "Now they have chosen a different way. A better way." She exchanged a look with her husband.

Zlata looked between them, feeling as if she had intruded on something private.

Zebedee met Zlata's gaze. "We returned this week from Caesarea Philippi."

She felt a spark of alarm. Had Taneli seen them on the road? Her father-in-law knew that their sons followed the rabbi from Nazareth. Would he trouble them if he knew of their visit? But what could he do? Parents had a right to see their children.

"We went to see James and John," Zebedee finished unnecessarily.

"And Yeshua," Salome said.

"And Yeshua," Zebedee echoed, a smile curving his mouth.

"Tell me." Zlata looked from Zebedee to Salome and back again. "Tell me everything you can."

Salome touched the back of Zlata's hand. "You know, don't you? You know who He is."

"Yes." Tears welled in Zlata's eyes. Breathlessly, she answered, "He is the Messiah."

Zebedee nodded. "Yeshua asked His disciples much the same question. He asked them, 'Who do people say that the Son of Man is?' And some answered with what we have all heard before. John the Baptist returned. Elijah and Jeremiah. One of the other prophets. Then He asked, 'But who do *you* say that I am?' And Simon answered Him, 'You are the Messiah, the Son of the living God.'"

Zlata's breath caught in her chest. "The Son of the living God," she whispered.

Zebedee leaned toward her. "And Yeshua said to him, 'Blessed are you, Simon son of Jonah, because flesh and blood did not reveal this to you, but My Father who is in heaven.'"

"You were there?" Zlata asked. "You heard it yourself?"

"No. We weren't there. Yeshua often goes away with just His twelve closest disciples. There are always many other disciples nearby, but He seeks time apart with the twelve. It was James who told us later what transpired."

"But that is not the most exciting part," Salome said. "Not long after that, perhaps a week, Yeshua took Simon and our

James and John up to a high mountain. Only the four of them were there. None of the others." She looked at her husband. "You tell her, Zebedee. The way John told you."

He nodded. "They were there on the high mountain, and suddenly the Master was transformed before them. His face shone like the sun, and His garments became as white as light. John said he saw two other men with Yeshua. Then Simon said something about tabernacles. I'm not quite sure what that was about. But this I remember." Zebedee's eyes took on a faraway look. "That was when a bright cloud overshadowed them and a voice came from it, saying, 'This is My beloved Son, with whom I am well-pleased; listen to Him!' And John said he and James and Simon fell on their faces, terrified."

A weighty silence fell over the three of them by the lake, as surely as it must have fallen over the men with Yeshua on that mountain.

Zlata clasped her hands together, her head bowed. How was it possible that anyone could survive in His presence? He was God's own beloved Son. John the Baptist had called Him the Lamb of God who takes away the sin of the world. To do so, He had to be sinless and spotless. How was it possible that sinners could approach Him? Sinners like Zlata, who had harbored bitterness and fear and resentment, who had forsaken prayer, who had lacked faith.

Adonai, forgive me.

"We have waited our whole lives for this day," Zebedee said in a reverent voice. "Our people have waited hundreds upon hundreds of years for the coming of the Messiah. Think of how privileged we are." He took hold of his wife's hand, who in turn took hold of Zlata's. "We have all seen Him with our own eyes."

Zlata blinked back more tears. "With our own eyes," she echoed softly.

"Well." Zebedee slapped his thigh with his free hand. "We must go home." He drew his wife to her feet. "It was good to see you, Zlata, daughter of Ira."

"It was good to see you, Zebedee. Salome."

Still holding hands, the couple walked away, going back along the lakeshore the way they had come.

Zlata sat still, recalling all that they'd shared with her, going over every detail in her mind, wanting to remember every word for the remainder of her life. She would share it with Bilhah, when next she saw her friend.

She also wished she could share what she'd heard with Joel, but it had been well over a month since she'd last seen Taneli's steward. Joel hadn't come to see his master in all those weeks, and Taneli hadn't sent Zlata with any messages either. Surely that would change soon, and she would be able to share about Yeshua's time in Phoenicia and Caesarea Philippi. Perhaps he would have other stories to share with her as well.

"We have waited our whole lives for this day."

"I will tell him," she said aloud. "As soon as I see Joel again, I will tell him everything I was told so he'll know how privileged he is as well."

Smiling, she rose and began the walk home.

CHAPTER TWENTY-THREE

Midsummer heat blanketed Capernaum as Zlata worked at the mill in the courtyard, grinding wheat. Sweat trickled down her spine, and she wished she could pause long enough to brush it away. A fly buzzed somewhere nearby.

"Keziah has asked for your help again," Abra announced from the doorway.

Startled by the words breaking the quiet of the courtyard, Zlata looked up. "My lady?"

"My cousin. She wants you to go to her."

"Is she ill?"

"She didn't say. Finish that, then go."

"Am I to stay with her?"

Abra flicked her hand in dismissal. "I suppose. If she can't afford a servant of her own, she shouldn't ask for one of—" She broke off and turned into the house.

Zlata resisted the urge to smile, in case her mother-in-law glanced back. She didn't want Abra to know how happy this unexpected request made her.

She resumed grinding, no longer minding the intense heat of the afternoon. Soon she would be on her way to Bethsaida to see Keziah. She hoped the older woman wasn't ill or injured again, but she couldn't think of any other reason for Keziah to send for her. Knowing this made her work even faster. She wanted to be done and on her way.

Half an hour later, she stepped through the courtyard door and onto the path that led to the public road. She didn't have to fight any crowds on her way to Bethsaida. Yeshua hadn't returned to Capernaum in weeks, although stories of more healings and miracles and the rabbi's teachings about the kingdom of God had reached them from Phoenicia and Decapolis, among other places. Now, Yeshua was reportedly in the vicinity of Magdala, to the south of Capernaum. Taneli and Nathan had gone there that morning, hoping to find a way to challenge or discredit the teacher. They had failed in that mission when they'd gone north in the spring. They would likely fail again this time. Still, that didn't dissuade them.

No breeze reached her with cooler air. The water itself was still as glass, the fishing vessels in the middle of the lake not seeming to move at all.

As she walked, Zlata remembered going out in the boat with her father when she was little. She had been about five or six years old. "You must do as I say," he'd told her as he lifted her over the side. "And you must stay out of the way."

Oh, how special she'd felt as she sat in the bow, watching her father and the other men push away from the shore.

At some point, the rocking of the boat and the fresh lake air had lulled her into sleep. It had been the shouts of the men as they'd brought in the catch that had awakened her. Fish, bouncing and writhing as some fell out of the net into the bottom of the boat. The sight of so many fish had frightened her a little. But she hadn't ever told her father. What fisherman's daughter wanted to admit to being afraid of fish?

She stopped walking and stared out over the water, her thoughts shifting to Yeshua, as they so often did.

After the feeding of the five thousand in the spring, she'd been told, the rabbi had sent His disciples across the lake while He went to pray by Himself. The boat had been headed for Gennesaret, a village to the south of Capernaum. Thus, she might have seen it if she'd been standing where she was today. But the winds had been contrary, unlike now, and their boat had been battered by the waves.

Then, the story went, at about the fourth watch, the darkness only broken by the lights in the night sky, Yeshua had come walking to His disciples on the sea. The men had been terrified, thinking He was a ghost.

She imagined herself in the bow of her father's boat, peeking over the side and seeing it for herself through the eyes of a small child. Her pulse quickened as she envisioned Yeshua's tunic blowing out behind Him in the wind, a ghostly figure, His sandaled feet skimming the top of the water.

"Take courage," Yeshua had said to them, "it is I; do not be afraid."

Zlata placed a hand over her heart.

"Lord," Simon, the one the Messiah called Cephas, had replied, "if it is You, command me to come to You on the water."

And Yeshua had told him to come.

Simon had gotten out of the boat, and he too walked on the water. But then he had taken his eyes off the rabbi, and he'd grown frightened. He'd started to sink. "Lord, save me!"

Lord, save me! her heart seemed to echo.

And immediately Yeshua had stretched out His hand for Simon, saving him.

It was said that as the rabbi and His disciple stepped into the boat, the wind instantly died down. Perhaps the sea had become as glassy as it was this very moment. Zlata imagined the water reflecting moonlight across its calm surface and drew in a shaky breath. Oh, if only she could have seen it for herself.

A dog's bark, the *baa* of a sheep, and the tinkling sound of a bell intruded on her thoughts. She turned from the lake to look in the opposite direction. A shepherd and a small flock of sheep were winding their way higher into the hills. She glanced up at the sky, realizing how late the hour was growing. This was no time to dawdle. Keziah must be watching for her, hopeful that she would arrive in time to help with the evening meal.

Keziah was, indeed, watching for Zlata's arrival. In fact, the older woman stood by her gate, looking up the road. When Zlata came into view, she raised her arm in an enthusiastic wave.

"Abra gave you leave to come," she called as Zlata drew closer.

"Yes. I am to stay as long as you need me. At least, she didn't say otherwise."

Keziah appeared neither injured nor sick. Her smile, brightening her face, said just the opposite.

"She didn't know why you sent for me," Zlata added.

"I sent for you because I wanted to see you. I've missed you, my daughter."

A sliver of alarm sounded in Zlata's head. Her mother-in-law had better not find out the real reason. "Abra thought you needed a servant for some reason. She was not happy about sending me."

"I can always use help. I grow old, and seeing to my daily needs can be too much at times. You cared for me with such tenderness when you were with me before. Why shouldn't I want you here?"

"But you are well?"

"I am well. Tired, at times, but still well." She motioned Zlata forward with a wave of her hand. "And I am hungry. Let us prepare our meager supper, and we can talk about what has happened since my visit to Capernaum."

A year had passed since Keziah's accident that precipitated Zlata's first stay in Bethsaida. Yet when Zlata stepped inside the small house, it felt as if only a few days had passed. The look of the room hadn't changed. The same scents lingered in the air. Even the light falling through the doorway felt familiar.

Over a meal of dried fish, bread, and fruit, Keziah peppered Zlata with questions. First she asked about Taneli and Abra, but she soon moved on to the subject of Yeshua, her interest keen.

"I arrive too late at the well each day," she said. "Those women who might tell me what they've heard about the rabbi have come and gone, and I return home knowing nothing more. So tell me what you have heard since we were last together."

Zlata shared everything she could remember, stories gleaned at the Capernaum well and in the marketplace, others overheard from Taneli as he and Nathan and Simon sat in the courtyard, plotting and complaining. She even shared what Zebedee had told her after his and Salome's visit to the north.

"What does Joel think of all this?"

Zlata's heart stuttered. "I haven't seen Joel since you came to visit."

"You haven't?" Keziah drew back, her eyes wide with disbelief. "Why not?"

Zlata shook her head. "I suppose he is too busy with his work in the vineyard."

"That doesn't sound likely. He works long and hard, but he made time to see you in the past. I know he did. I saw it. Maybe Taneli learned of his interest in you and put a stop to it."

The suggestion caused conflicting emotions to swirl inside Zlata. Conflicting but not unfamiliar. For many weeks, she'd felt the same confusion whenever she thought about Joel. But only now did she realize how deeply she'd missed their long talks. Even more this spring and summer than during the previous winter when Taneli had forbidden her and Abra to leave the house without him. Perhaps it hurt more because she enjoyed some freedom again and still he hadn't found a way to meet with her the way they used to. It hadn't occurred to her that his absence might be because of her father-in-law. Not even after Dara's comment that day by the stream. Had Taneli truly noticed the growing friendship between Zlata and his steward? And if so, had he then made certain it didn't continue?

"I've upset you," Keziah said, her voice gentle.

"No." But even as she said the word, tears welled in her eyes.

"I'm sorry."

"You did nothing wrong." Zlata blinked back the tears. "I…I don't know why I'm reacting this way."

"Don't you? Zlata, you are still a young woman. You should not be shut away from life. Taneli has not done right by you since the death of your husband."

"He gave me a home." The lie tasted bitter on her tongue.

"He gave you shelter and work. He didn't give you a home."

Zlata shook her head again, although her heart agreed.

"You could come to live with me," Keziah said softly. "I have little, but what I have I would gladly share with you. And you would be free to see whom you want when you want."

This time, Zlata's tears couldn't be stopped. They flowed down her cheeks, overwhelmed by the love she felt for Keziah and by the kindness the woman had shown toward her. Still, there was a tug of reluctance to accept. Capernaum had always been her home. She knew the people in the marketplace and the women at the well. She recognized the fishermen who'd worked with her father. There were countless memories of her childhood and girlhood everywhere in the town and the surrounding countryside. There were memories of Yerik and the love they had once shared. Would she want to be so far from all of that?

"I have nothing of my own to offer you in return," she said at last.

"I want nothing." Keziah's hand covered hers. "Pray about it. Adonai will show you what to do."

Zlata nodded. "I will pray about it."

CHAPTER TWENTY-FOUR

Early the next morning, after fetching water from the well in Bethsaida, Zlata walked into the hills beyond the village. It was the area where Yeshua was said to have fed the five thousand men with only a few loaves and fishes. It was also where the rabbi was said to have withdrawn to pray on His own before He walked on the water.

She imagined Him in these hills with His disciples and with thousands of other people, so many trying to get close to Him, hoping to be touched by Him, wanting to be healed by Him. It wasn't difficult for her to imagine it, having seen the huge crowds that had followed Him when He was in and near Capernaum. There would have been some who were merely curious. There would have been others, like Taneli, who wanted only to discredit Him. While Yeshua had a voice that rang with authority, still it would have been impossible for everyone among the thousands to hear Him. Certainly not those on the farthest fringes. Bits and pieces would have been passed along through the crowd to satisfy them.

Zlata settled onto a large rock. For a long time, she simply listened to the silence surrounding her. There was no breeze this morning. There were no sheep on the hillsides, no one else seeking solitude. Only quiet.

At last she closed her eyes and began to pray. "Hear, O Israel! The Lord our God is one Lord."

From her earliest memories, her mother and father had begun and ended their days with the repeating of the Shema. With these words, they had opened their times of prayer. With these words, they had declared their love for and obedience to the one God. As Zlata whispered the words now, she did the same. Then she turned her confusion over to the Lord.

What would Adonai have her do about Keziah's offer? It seemed simple enough on the surface. She would have more freedom in the older woman's home. She would know kindness. But Keziah was a widow without unending resources. If Zlata came to live with her, would it actually injure Keziah in the future? Would Zlata be taking advantage of her hospitality? Would Keziah's daughter object to the arrangement? Might it even cause a break between Keziah and Abra, the only member of Keziah's family who lived nearby?

"You will make known to me the path of life."

She needed clarity above all else. Perhaps part of her confusion was caused by how few choices she'd had for much of her life. She had gone where she was told to go, done what she was told to do, lived where she was told to live. Having a choice now seemed to paralyze her.

"He guides me in the paths of righteousness for His name's sake."

Looking back, Zlata believed God had used the weeks she'd spent with Keziah the previous year as part of the healing in her heart. In Keziah's home, she had realized that she wasn't unloved or unlovable. Believing that lie had twisted her thinking and fanned the flames of her bitterness. Was more healing awaiting her if she came to live in Bethsaida?

"Make me know Your ways, O Lord; teach me Your paths."

And what of Joel? If Keziah was right, if Taneli had objected to Zlata's friendship with the steward of his vineyards, then perhaps living in Bethsaida would allow her to see him again, talk to him again. Whether or not there would be anything more between them, their friendship could continue.

"The Lord is compassionate and gracious, slow to anger and abounding in lovingkindness."

Peace seemed to expand her heart, and she knew what she would do. She would accept the gracious offer. She would make Bethsaida her new home. She would start a new life here with Keziah.

Keziah received Zlata's news with great joy and promised that the two of them would go together to see Taneli. "But not yet, my daughter. I am feeling tired and am not up to that walk. It is too far and too hot for such a journey. Perhaps we'll go next week. Abra won't be expecting you before then anyway."

Zlata was in no hurry for a confrontation—if it would be that—with her father-in-law. It changed nothing if she and Keziah waited a week before telling her in-laws that she was going to live with Keziah permanently. Zlata had very little in Taneli's house anyway. Her clothes she had with her. But there was a blue scarf and the two coins from Yerik wrapped in it. Those she didn't want to lose.

"Perhaps we should have a celebration, you and I," Keziah said. "Some roasted lamb, perhaps, to add to the vegetable stew. Tomorrow we'll go to the marketplace early and find a choice piece of meat for our supper."

"As you wish. Why don't you rest, and I will prepare our supper."

Keziah didn't object. In fact, she made her way outside into the shade, leaving Zlata to find what she needed for their evening meal. It didn't take long before she carried the items out to the fire. When she glanced toward her friend, she found her fast asleep. Something about the way Keziah looked caused Zlata to pause in her meal preparations.

Yesterday, Keziah had insisted that there was nothing wrong with her, that she had sent for Zlata only because she wanted company, not because she was unwell. But this morning, Zlata wondered if that was the whole truth. Her friend did seem unusually tired.

When their vegetable stew started to simmer over the fire, Zlata rose and checked on Keziah. The older woman still slept. Rather than disturb her, Zlata went inside and did some tidying, making note of what they needed to purchase in the marketplace in addition to the lamb Keziah wanted to buy for their two-person celebration.

As she swept the floor, Zlata sang a song her mother had taught her when she was only a girl, the words bringing back pleasant memories. This too could be a happy home. She and

Keziah would do well together. Zlata was young and strong. Keziah was wise and caring. They would be a family, the family neither of them had had in a long while. Together they could do what one alone could not.

Thanksgiving rose in Zlata's heart as she poured water from the jar into a cup. After drinking it, she refilled it and carried it outside for Keziah.

Only Keziah wasn't thirsty. She would never be thirsty again.

Zlata mourned for her friend with tears and wailing. Neighbors and friends joined her with loud cries of their own, but she scarcely noticed them. Her sorrow was deep and personal.

Abra and Taneli arrived, having received Zlata's urgently sent message, and Abra helped Zlata wash and wrap the body in grave clothes. Zlata covered her friend's precious face with the *sudarium*. The women sprinkled the white cloths with aromatic crystals of balm, making the air in the small house smell sweet. Afterward, they placed Keziah's body on a litter, then followed as friends carried the litter to the burial place located on the outskirts of Bethsaida, as prescribed by law. Reverently, they laid the woman's remains to rest as the sun grew low in the western sky.

When Zlata returned to Capernaum with her in-laws, her heart was in tatters. She had dared to hope for a new happiness, but it had been snatched from her before it could begin.

Knowing she wouldn't see Keziah's smile again or that impish twinkle in her eyes, knowing she wouldn't hear Keziah say "my daughter" in that loving tone of hers or listen to her soft snores as they lay on their mats at night left her with an emptiness she hadn't expected to feel again. While Keziah's death didn't revive bitterness in Zlata's heart, it did leave her lonely.

CHAPTER TWENTY-FIVE

Aweek after her return to Capernaum, Zlata made her way to the stream late one morning, the air hot and still.

She sank onto the bank and stared down at the water trickling by. It had been difficult to focus her thoughts ever since the moment she'd discovered Keziah, and it remained so today. But Abra seemed willing to leave Zlata to herself, letting her mourn in her own way, not caring when she wandered off by herself, and for that Zlata was grateful.

Now, closing her eyes, she tried to pray, but the words wouldn't form. So she allowed herself to simply sit without effort, without expectation.

"Zlata."

Her pulse jumped at the sound of Joel's voice. Tears welled and rolled down her cheeks.

"Dara told me I would find you here."

She opened her eyes and looked to her right, watching as he stepped to the stream and sat on the ground a few feet away from her.

"I'm sorry," he said. "I only heard about Keziah last night. I came as soon as I could."

Zlata nodded.

"Keziah was a good friend to you. She cared for you a great deal."

"Yes," she managed to say around the lump in her throat.

"I've missed seeing you."

She nodded, hoping he would know it meant she had missed him too.

"I could not come when I wanted."

Somehow, his simple statement convinced her that Keziah had been right about his reason for staying away. Not wanting to dwell on it, she asked, "What have you learned of Yeshua?"

His expression held both tenderness and excitement. "I don't understand how anyone can doubt that He's the Messiah, the Anointed One we have awaited for generations. He is not all that we have been taught He will be. For one, He is not a great political leader. Not yet anyway. But He is descended from King David. He is well versed in the law. He does make righteous decisions. He performs miracles for all to see. He *is* the Messiah. I wish everyone could know it."

Her heart thrummed as she looked at Joel, for she believed all that he said. Even her current sorrow couldn't stop her from believing.

Joel was silent for a short while, the delight draining from his eyes. In a softer voice, he continued, "It's said that now He teaches His disciples that He must go to Jerusalem, where He will suffer many things at the hands of the elders and chief priests." A frown furrowed his forehead. "He speaks of being killed and then raised up on the third day."

"Killed?"

"Yes."

"How can that be?" she whispered. "The Messiah cannot be killed before He completes all that was spoken of Him."

"And then He told a crowd, 'If anyone wishes to come after Me, he must deny himself, and take up his cross and follow Me.'"

Zlata sucked in her breath. "A cross?" Images of Rome's preferred means of torture and death rushed into her mind. She had seen a cross with a man hanging on it only once, from a distance, when she'd gone with her parents to Jerusalem, and it was a sight she would never forget. She understood the horror of it, as did all her people.

"He said," Joel continued, "'For whoever wishes to save his life will lose it; but whoever loses his life for My sake and the gospel's will save it.'"

One of the things Taneli feared was that Yeshua, with His great popularity among the people, would try to raise up an army, and that, in turn, would bring the heel of Rome down upon the necks of all in Israel. In a secret part of Zlata's heart, she had hoped for that army. She longed to see their oppressors driven from the land. She wanted to see the men responsible for Yerik's death punished, defeated, perhaps killed themselves. Wasn't that what she had been taught would happen when Messiah came at last? That He would drive out their enemies and take the throne? That all Israel would be free forever.

Yet that wasn't what Yeshua seemed to teach about Himself.

"I need to see Him," she said. "I want to hear Him teach again. When will He return to Capernaum, do you think?"

"I don't know. He and His men have traveled all about these many months. He has been here but leaves quickly, going north and east and south. The crowds are not as great as before, but there are still many who seek Him out."

Zlata leaned toward Joel. "Will you make sure, when Yeshua is nearby again, that I know of it?"

His frown returned.

"You do not need to take me, Joel. I won't let Taneli know you've had any part of it. But I must see Yeshua again. I must. And others might not let me know when He is near."

Joel released a sigh. "I will make sure you know, Zlata. I promise you."

Tears welled in her eyes again. "Thank you," she whispered before turning her blurry gaze back upon the water.

A short while later, she heard him rise and walk away. It wasn't until he was gone that she remembered she hadn't shared what Zebedee and Salome told her.

Next time. Next time I see him, I'll tell him.

Able to focus her mind on at least one thing, Zlata prayed for Yeshua's return to Capernaum and for an opportunity to slip away to see Him when He came. She prayed for it every morning and every evening. She prayed for it when she walked to the well or sat by the stream or stood on the rooftop, staring out at the Sea of Galilee.

Taneli rarely met with his friends in the courtyard in the days and weeks following Keziah's death. He was often gone from home, and when he returned, he seldom talked to anyone in the household, not even his wife. His anger remained, but it seemed to be at a low boil.

Joel's words rang in Zlata's memory: *"He teaches His disciples that He must go to Jerusalem, where He will suffer many things at the hands of the elders and chief priests."*

Elders and chief priests. Men like Taneli.

Fear for Yeshua mingled with mourning for Keziah as Zlata awaited the answer to her prayers.

CHAPTER TWENTY-SIX

It was, perhaps, one answer to Zlata's prayers that Taneli's household had grown used to her wandering off at various times of the day, that they no longer expected her to be working in the garden or tending to meal preparations, always within the sound of their voices.

Early one morning, as summer drew to a close, Joel came for her. Zlata was once again seated beside the stream, the water barely a trickle now. Hearing his approach, she looked up and knew at once why he had come. She scrambled to her feet, securing her headscarf in place as she did so.

"The rabbi is in the hills to the north of the sea." He held out a hand toward her. "Come. We should hurry if we want to be near enough to hear Him for ourselves."

Her heart quickened in excitement as she moved to walk beside Joel. They followed the path toward the western shore of the lake. Once there, they would be out of sight of Taneli's house, even should someone stand on the roof and look in that direction.

It wasn't long before she saw a familiar sight—people filling the road, all headed in the same direction. Pilgrims from far away. A blind man led by the hand. A boy with a withered leg, on crutches. A woman, large with child, riding in the back of a donkey cart. And a few Pharisees in their distinctive attire.

Zlata tugged her headscarf forward, hoping to hide her face from view. She hadn't recognized the men, but that didn't mean they wouldn't know Taneli and possibly her. Joel must have noticed them too, for he moved to her other side, putting himself between her and the Pharisees.

Zlata and Joel walked quickly, weaving their way between slower travelers. It wasn't until the road into Capernaum merged with the one they were on that she began to see a few familiar faces here and there. She pulled the headscarf even closer around her face. As much as she wanted to see and hear Yeshua for herself, she also didn't want to be recognized by her neighbors.

Up ahead of them, people had begun to leave the road, climbing the hillside.

"This way," Joel said, and he took her hand, pulling her along with him.

The crowd surged on while Joel and Zlata made their way alone.

"I know these hills," he said. "We'll come up and around on the far side."

Zlata glanced behind. No one had followed them. The fear of recognition drained away for the moment, and she released her grasp on the scarf, not needing to hide her face for the moment.

Joel was used to tramping up and down hillsides in the vineyard. His legs and arms were strong from heavy labor. To Zlata it seemed he was more like a mountain goat than a man as he traversed the hillside, his hand grasping hers tightly. At last they reached the top. It fell away almost at once, and there, opposite them on a second hillside stood Yeshua, speaking to His disciples and the followers who had already joined them.

"It must be difficult for Him to ever find a moment alone," Zlata said as they began their descent.

Joel moved more slowly now, making sure neither of them slipped or stumbled on their way down. Then he led her to a large olive tree. The valley between the two hillsides seemed to have been shaped for the purpose of carrying Yeshua's voice straight to Joel and Zlata as they settled on the ground, their backs against the tree, their faces shaded from the morning sun.

"What do you think?" Yeshua asked in a loud voice as His gaze swept the increasing crowd. "If any man has a hundred sheep, and one of them has gone astray, does he not leave the ninety-nine on the mountains and go and search for the one that is straying?"

Zlata soaked in the sound of His voice, her heart quickening. How could anyone hear Him and not know that He was the Messiah? He was humble, a carpenter by trade, yet there was something majestic about Him that was irrefutable. Why did men like Taneli seek to silence Him? He was a man of peace, and He taught everyone to love.

Thinking of her father-in-law, she looked away from Yeshua toward the people sitting and standing around Him. After a while, she found some Pharisees standing on the far side of the crowd near another olive tree. There were six in all. Perhaps some were the men she had seen on the road, but they were too far away to recognize. Still, she felt the need to pull her headscarf forward once again.

"Again I say to you…"

She looked back at Yeshua, at the kindness in His face, the compassion in His eyes, so clear even from where she sat.

"…that if two of you agree on earth about anything that they may ask, it shall be done for them by My Father who is in heaven. For where two or three have gathered together in My name, I am there in their midst."

She thought of the times she and Joel had sat together and talked about Yeshua and wrestled with the words He'd spoken. How wonderful if He could have been there with them, seated in their midst. The image in her mind caused her to smile.

Yeshua talked on, sharing the meaning of forgiveness with a parable she hadn't heard before. She knew the teacher wanted her to forgive those who had hurt her. He'd taught about forgiveness many times. Even the prayer Bilhah had shared with her expressed His wishes.

"And his lord," Yeshua concluded, "moved with anger, handed him over to the torturers until he should repay all that was owed him. My heavenly Father will also do the same to you, if each of you does not forgive his brother from your heart."

She noticed some people rise and leave the area, and her breath caught. She'd done the same thing the first time she'd heard Yeshua teach.

"Blessed are those who mourn," He'd said on that long ago day, *"for they shall be comforted.… Blessed are the merciful, for they shall receive mercy.… You are the salt of the earth; but if the salt has become*

tasteless, how can it be made salty again?... But I say to you, love your enemies and pray for those who persecute you."

His words had been too much for her then. She'd run from them. She'd run from Him. She'd been so wrong.

She looked after those who were departing and wanted to cry out for them to stay, to listen some more, to open their ears and their hearts. If they would only give Yeshua a chance, they would discover the truth. That He was the Anointed One, sent by God.

She looked toward the rabbi again, not wanting to miss a word.

Zlata parted from Joel on the road near the entrance to the vineyard.

"Are you sure?" he asked, a frown creasing his brow. "I can see you back to the house."

"No. You have done enough. Thank you, Joel. Thank you for this day. I will remember it forever."

He looked up and down the road. It was filled with people headed to their homes and campsites. The road wasn't as crowded as it had been that morning, but it was still busy. He seemed to debate whether or not she would be safe.

"It isn't that far. I will be fine."

As if to prove her point, she heard someone call her name. Turning, she saw Bilhah moving toward her. "You were there today," her friend said.

"We were there," Zlata answered, glancing back at Joel.

"I'm so glad." She clasped Zlata's hand. "I was sorry to hear about Keziah. I know you loved her."

"Yes."

Bilhah lowered her voice. "The Master is leaving Galilee, and I intend to go with Him."

"Bilhah!"

"I have met the women who serve Him. They have welcomed me into their midst as one of His disciples. I will go with them to Judea."

It surprised Zlata how much it hurt to think she might not ever see Bilhah again. Their meetings over the past year had been infrequent and brief, but still they had been important to her. Selfishly, she didn't want to let go of another friendship. It felt like one loss too many, especially so soon after Keziah.

"Let us walk together," Bilhah said.

Zlata looked again in Joel's direction. He offered a nod and a brief smile.

Bilhah hooked her arm through Zlata's and soon they were part of the stream of people flowing back toward Capernaum. On the way, Zlata shared all that had transpired in Bethsaida and in the weeks since. She hadn't told anyone else about Keziah's invitation for Zlata to live with her. She was glad she could share it with Bilhah.

When they reached the pathway to Taneli's house, they stepped out of the way of others to say their goodbyes.

"I will pray for you, Zlata," Bilhah said, taking her hand a second time.

"Thank you. And I, you."

"I believe in my heart that I will see you again."

"I hope you're right. I will miss you."

Bilhah leaned forward and kissed Zlata's cheek. "Peace be with you." She turned and walked away. It was a bit like another death, seeing her friend leave, and the pain caused Zlata to turn and hurry up the path.

She hadn't thought to find Taneli standing not far beyond the courtyard doorway. She hadn't thought to be cautious about her return to the house. In her excitement over all she'd heard Yeshua teach and her sorrow over saying goodbye to Bilhah, she'd forgotten everything else.

"Where have you been?" Taneli demanded.

He didn't need her to tell him. He already knew. She could see it in his blazing eyes. She answered him anyway. "I—I went to see the rabbi."

She cried out when the back of his hand knocked her against the wall.

"I warned you." He stepped toward her. "You were told not to follow Him."

"I wanted to see for—"

He struck her again. Her head snapped back, bouncing off the wall. Her headscarf slipped to her shoulders, and he took hold of her by the hair, pulling her with him toward the house. She cried out again, struggling against him, begging him to let her go, to have mercy.

But there was no mercy in Taneli.

PART III

Spring, during the final month of Yeshua's Judean ministry

As Jesus was about to go up to Jerusalem, He took the twelve disciples aside by themselves, and on the way He said to them, "Behold, we are going up to Jerusalem; and the Son of Man will be delivered to the chief priests and scribes, and they will condemn Him to death, and will hand Him over to the Gentiles to mock and scourge and crucify Him, and on the third day He will be raised up."

—Matthew 20:17–19, NASB

CHAPTER TWENTY-SEVEN

Yeshua and His disciples had departed Galilee for Judea not long after Zlata went with Joel to listen to the rabbi teach in the Capernaum hillsides one last time. It had been many weeks after that before Zlata learned Joel had left as well, having been dismissed as Taneli's steward. The news made another wound in her already broken spirit.

Capernaum had become the quiet town it was before Yeshua made it the hub for His ministry. Strangers had ceased camping in droves along the roadsides or near the lake, and the women seen at the well, once Zlata had returned to her chores, were familiar to her. One season turned into another—summer becoming autumn, autumn becoming winter, and finally winter becoming spring—without her noticing.

When Taneli announced that Zlata would accompany him and Abra to Jerusalem for Passover, Zlata didn't ask why. She'd learned, at last, not to question anything her father-in-law told her. Perhaps he was taking her because he wanted to teach her another lesson about obedience. Both to him and to God. Perhaps he didn't trust her to be left behind as he'd done in years past. Whatever the reason, she would visit the holy city again for the Feast of Unleavened Bread—and that put a little spark of hope into her heart. Hope that she might see Yeshua again.

Taneli had done his best to cut off all news from beyond Galilee. His best hadn't been good enough. Zlata had still heard stories about the rabbi. She'd learned that Yeshua had been in Jerusalem for the Feast of Tabernacles, and He'd been there again for the Feast of Dedication. Stories of more healings and other miracles had reached her ears as well, though none so amazing as the one about Him raising His friend from the grave in Bethany.

I want to see Him again, she thought as she readied the donkey for the journey early in the morning. *If only I could see Him again.*

Wisdom told her not to hope for such a thing, but still she hoped it. Just a glimpse would be enough. She also hoped she might see Bilhah. She didn't allow herself to wonder about Joel. She had no idea where he was. Had he found work in another vineyard in Galilee? Perhaps on the other side of the lake. Or had he gone far away? Gone forever. Like so many from her life.

The donkey looked at her as she carried the last of the supplies for their journey toward it and placed the items into the baskets hanging over its sides. Then she returned to her room for her own few possessions, including the two coins from Yerik that were still wrapped in the blue headscarf. After placing them in the sack she carried over one shoulder, she went outside and was waiting when Taneli stepped through the courtyard doorway, Abra following in his wake.

The journey to Jerusalem would take many days, and much of it would be through arduous terrain. Today, they would follow the major Roman road that skirted the Sea of Galilee. Then they would head off in the direction of Perea, for Taneli would never travel through Samaria. Unthinkable for a Pharisee, even though that route to Jerusalem was much shorter. Other pilgrims would also be on the road, headed for the same destination, and Taneli's small group would join up with them until they were many. Hopefully enough to discourage robbers and thieves who might think of them as easy prey.

Holding a walking stick, Taneli set out, expecting the womenfolk and servants to keep up without being told to do so. He didn't speak to anyone. He walked with purpose, head held high. The fringe of his upper garment, enlarged as was the custom of the Pharisees, bounced and danced with every deliberate step. At the proper times, he stopped to say his prescribed prayers, and Zlata and the others stopped and waited until he was ready to move along. Chanan, the young man who cared for Taneli's livestock, led the donkey, and Zlata followed behind the animal, preferring the distance between herself and her in-laws. Out of their sight, she was less apt to do something to displease them.

For much of the day, she could see boats bobbing on the lake, sunlight glinting off the surface. A breeze carried refreshing air from the water, making their walk more tolerable. They bought fish from a merchant before they made camp for the night. By then, their party had grown to fifteen people.

They broke their fast the following morning before setting out again, the Sea of Galilee now behind them. By midmorning a young girl, perhaps ten years of age, from one of the other families, fell into step beside Zlata.

"I'm Ruth." Excitement glimmered in her eyes.

"Shalom, Ruth." She smiled briefly. "I'm Zlata."

"We're going to Jerusalem. Are you?"

"Yes."

"I've never been before. Have you?"

"Yes."

"Is it as big as they say?"

"It's big. There are many, many people."

"And the temple. Did you see it too?"

Zlata nodded, remembering when she had been there with her parents.

"Is it as beautiful as my father says?"

"It is very beautiful. Very big and very beautiful. It towers over everything else. Even the king's palace."

"We're going to stay with my mother's sister for Passover. Her husband is a potter."

Zlata smiled and nodded again, realizing more participation than that wasn't necessary.

"My father is a shepherd. His brother is caring for the flock while we're away." Ruth pointed toward a man walking some distance ahead of Taneli. "Father says we must keep watch for bandits. They know there are many of us going to Jerusalem for the festival, and we must be careful."

"Your father is wise, and he looks quite strong. I'm glad he is with us."

"He will protect you and your master. He will protect us all."

Zlata looked at Taneli's back. Beneath those robes was a man with greater strength than the little girl knew. Strength enough to— She closed her eyes for a couple of steps, banishing the memories.

"I've seen my father drive off a lion when it was after the flock," Ruth continued, pride in her voice. "Mother says he wields his staff like a sword."

Zlata drew a breath and spoke of happier times. "My father was a fisherman. He could make a heavy net fly far out into the water with a toss." She moved her arms, mimicking the motion as she remembered it.

"Does he still fish?"

"No." She shook her head. "He died."

Ruth's face fell and her voice softened. "I'm sorry."

"Thank you."

"Ruth." A woman came walking from the opposite direction, her eyes searching this way and that until they landed on the girl. "Ruth. There you are." She looked at Zlata. "Has my daughter been troubling you?"

"Not at all."

"This is Zlata," Ruth said, smiling again. "Her father was a fisherman."

"I'm Devorah, the wife of Ehud." She turned and walked beside her daughter, the girl reaching out to take her hand.

Zlata had been content with silence all of the previous day. She was used to her own company, her own thoughts. But now she took pleasure in this exchange. Devorah was a stranger. She didn't know Zlata's history or her complicated relationship with Taneli and Abra. Devorah, no doubt, thought her only a servant in the household. Which she both was…and wasn't.

By early afternoon, the party had grown to a group of over twenty adults. When they stopped for a brief rest, Ruth, not seeming to be tired despite the miles covered already, went off to play with other children. Devorah was joined by her husband, and they settled on the ground in shade provided by an outcropping of rocks. Zlata went to tend to Abra's needs, taking with her some bread and dried fruit from the donkey's basket. She'd scarcely had time for a couple of bites herself before the travelers were on their way again.

One day followed another with relative sameness. They walked, they rested, they ate, they slept. They traversed narrow paths and climbed steep trails. They crossed the Jordan River one time as the road took them east, and on another day they crossed it again as the road took them west. They met more devout Jews on their way to Jerusalem. They watched for bandits and at one point had to clear off the road to make way for Roman soldiers marching toward the holy city.

And finally the day arrived when Jerusalem came into view.

As Zlata had done on her first visit to the holy city as a child, she did again now as a widow. She sang softly as they ascended toward the city. "Behold, bless the Lord, all servants of the Lord, who serve by night in the house of the Lord! Lift up your hands to the sanctuary and bless the Lord. May the Lord bless you from Zion, He who made heaven and earth."

When Zlata began a second song, Ruth's young voice joined in.

"Behold, how good and how pleasant it is for brothers to dwell together in unity!"

Next Devorah took up the words of praise, followed by Ehud, whose voice was deep and rich.

"It is like the precious oil upon the head, coming down upon the beard, even Aaron's beard, coming down upon the edge of his robes. It is like the dew of Hermon coming down upon the mountains of Zion; for there the LORD commanded the blessing—life forever."

Zlata felt renewed strength in her legs as she praised God with the others.

"Jerusalem?" Ruth asked when the song ended.

"Yes," her mother answered.

Ruth pointed. "And is that the temple?"

"Yes, my daughter." Devorah stroked Ruth's head. "It is." Then the woman looked at Zlata. "Are you staying in the city?"

Zlata nodded. "With a friend of Taneli's."

"I pray that your Passover will be a time of blessing."

"Thank you. And I pray the same for you." Zlata's gaze went toward Jerusalem again. They were drawing closer to the city gates, and the road had become much more crowded.

Ehud took hold of his wife's arm. "We must go this way." He motioned with his head.

Devorah, in turn, took hold of Ruth's hand. "Goodbye, my friend," Ruth said to Zlata. "Perhaps we will see each other again on the journey home."

"I would like that. Goodbye, Ruth. Goodbye, Devorah, Ehud."

She watched the little family break away and follow another road. Looking at them, she remembered again her first visit to Jerusalem. She and her parents must have looked very much like those three, trying to make their way through a sea of people.

CHAPTER TWENTY-EIGHT

Jerusalem was more than Zlata remembered. More of every-thing. More people. More noise. More smells. She had to remain vigilant lest she become separated from Taneli and Abra in the crowded, winding streets. While keeping her gaze locked on Taneli's turban, she also held on to the basket hanging from the donkey's side, somewhat comforted by the animal's familiar-ity even as she was jostled against it time and again.

"We're going to the Upper City," Chanan told her. "This Barukh, the master's friend, he must be a very wealthy man to live there."

A wealthy man indeed, Zlata thought when they arrived at their destination, a spacious villa with a view of much of the city. Barukh welcomed them to his home himself before taking Tan-eli and Abra away to another room for refreshments while Zlata was shown to the bedchamber where her in-laws would sleep. There, she put away the personal items they'd brought with them then sat on a cushion to await instructions. None came.

It was hunger that forced Zlata to leave the chamber and go in search of something to eat. But finding the kitchen wasn't easy. There were many rooms and hallways. She had always thought Taneli's house in Capernaum large, but it was a simple country cottage compared to this one. This house seemed more a palace, with its frescoed walls and mosaic floors. The extent of Barukh's wealth was beyond her comprehension, but one thing she knew for certain. The trader must be a religious Jew, or Taneli would never stay in the same house with him.

Eventually, she came upon a household servant who then showed her not only where to get her evening meal but to the servant quarters where she would sleep. That evening, she sat on her mat, waiting to be summoned to the bedchamber. No summons came. Finally, she lay down and drifted off to sleep.

Much to Zlata's surprise, neither of her in-laws seemed to care what she did while they were in Jerusalem. In the first days that followed their arrival, Barukh's wife entertained Abra during the day and the household servants tended to Abra's needs the rest of the time. As for Taneli, he left the house early each morning and didn't return until it was time for supper. Zlata learned all of this not from her in-laws but from other servants.

Finally, boredom drove her beyond the walls of Barukh's house. She explored the grounds, but nothing there held her interest. There was nothing to do but stare at the fountain, and she wasn't used to sitting still and doing nothing for lengthy periods of time.

She returned to the sleeping quarters and retrieved the sack that held the two coins and blue headscarf. Then she went outside, this time into the street.

Standing there, she got her bearings. From here she could see both Herod's palace complex with its three towers to her left and, on the opposite side of the city—much farther away—

the massive Temple Mount. With those two landmarks to guide her, she would surely be able to find her way back, no matter how deep she ventured into the city. It wasn't her intention to go far. She simply wanted some time outside, away from the villa where she felt so out of place and unnecessary.

Eventually, she found herself in a street of weavers, and she paused to look at the fine cloth that was offered for sale. Fingering some blue fabric, she thought of Bilhah and wondered where she was. Was she even now working inside a shop on this street, or did she continue to travel with the rabbi? Zlata wished she knew.

"He is coming!" a woman called at the far end of the street. "He is coming."

Zlata stepped back and looked toward the voice. Other people had stopped to stare in the same direction. A few left their shopping and hurried away.

Zlata's pulse quickened. "Who is coming?" she asked the woman next to her at the display.

"I don't know." With a huff, she went back to her shopping.

Zlata stepped into the middle of the street. It couldn't be. This wasn't Capernaum. This was a large city. Tens of thousands of people lived here. A hundred thousand, Taneli had once said. Thousands more were pouring into Jerusalem every day because of the approach of Passover. The shouting woman could have meant anyone. Anybody at all.

But what if it was Yeshua who was coming? Only He could stir that kind of excitement. She walked down the street, her footsteps quickening until she was almost running.

As had happened in Capernaum, she soon found herself joining the flow of people moving in the same direction. Excited voices sounded all around her as she was swept along this street and that, then finally taken beyond the walls of the city. The commotion was even more obvious on the approach to the city gate.

Then she heard the shouts. "Hosanna to the Son of David." Many voices were lifted in praise, repeating the words of the psalmist.

Yeshua!

She saw Him then, through a break in the crowd. It was Yeshua, riding on a donkey. People from the crowd were spreading their coats on the road. Others were laying down branches cut from the trees, covering the place where the animal would soon step. There was something regal about the way He sat upon the donkey, something knowing in His expression as He looked out at the rejoicing, noisy crowd.

"Blessed is He who comes in the name of the Lord."

Zlata blinked back tears. It was the Messiah riding into Jerusalem, as the prophet had promised. It was happening before her very eyes.

"Who is this?" someone behind her asked.

"It's the prophet Yeshua," someone else answered. "From Nazareth in Galilee."

It's Yeshua, her heart sang again. *It's Yeshua.*

She'd hoped she might find Him in Jerusalem, and here He was. She had seen Him. If only for a moment, she had seen Him. It was a miracle that Taneli hadn't been able to stop her from seeing Him. Hadn't even tried to stop her. In truth, Taneli seemed to have forgotten her since their arrival in the holy city.

People pushed their way forward, others wanting to see what Zlata had seen. The crowd closed in until she couldn't see the rabbi at all.

"Hosanna in the highest!"

Hands shoved her to the side. Another pair of hands caught her before she could topple. She lifted her gaze, thinking she would thank the man for his help, but he was still looking toward the road, watching Yeshua pass by, a look of wonder on his face. The crowd surged back toward the city gate.

Zlata didn't try to follow. It was enough for now that she had seen His arrival in Jerusalem. It was enough that she knew He was in the holy city for Passover. She stood still and allowed the throng to move on without her. Only when it had thinned to a steady trickle of people did she step toward the road again. Most of the cloaks had been reclaimed from the ground, but the branches still lay in the dirt, scattered about, trampled under hundreds of passing sandals. She stopped to pick up one of the branches and pressed it close to her chest, smiling.

"Hosanna in the highest," she whispered as she moved onward. "Hosanna in the highest."

Anah, a slave girl in Barukh's household, sat near Zlata that evening at supper. While other servants visited over the meal, Zlata and Anah ate in silence.

The stew and bread were nearly gone when Anah suddenly said, "You were outside the city gates today."

Zlata's pulse jumped as she looked at the girl.

"You haven't left this house since your master brought you here. You have stayed in these quarters. But today you wandered that far. Was it Him you went to see? The One on the donkey?"

"You followed me?" Although she formed the words as a question, somehow she was certain they were true.

Anah nodded.

"Why?"

The girl reached into a pocket and pulled out a mite. "For this."

"You were *paid* to follow me?" Her heart thudded. "Taneli."

Anah leaned close. "My master could have commanded I do it without reward. I am only a slave." She shrugged. "But it was good to receive payment."

"And you told Taneli where I went." Zlata remembered that joyous moment when she caught a glimpse of Yeshua through the multitude. She remembered the shouts of praise all around her as He rode toward the gates of Jerusalem. If Taneli knew she had been among that crowd, watching the rabbi's triumphal entrance, he would—

"Your master was told you went to the street of the weavers. He was told you liked the blue cloth especially." The girl grinned. "Perhaps when you go out tomorrow, he will be told about your favorite pots. There are many fine potters here in Jerusalem. I could give you directions to find their wares."

Confusion washed through Zlata. Did Anah mean she hadn't told Taneli where she'd gone after looking at the blue cloth, despite the coin he'd paid the slave? Did the girl mean she wouldn't tell him every place Zlata went tomorrow, no matter where that might be?

As if the questions had been asked aloud, Anah nodded, understanding in her eyes.

Zlata wanted to hug the girl. She'd felt lonely for many months. She hadn't known a kind act in ages. And suddenly this girl, this stranger, who knew no freedom of her own, had protected her. She wanted to repay her in some way. She had nothing to give. Except…except what she knew of Yeshua.

"Do you know who that was? The man on the donkey who caused such excitement."

Anah shook her head.

"His name is Yeshua. He is a rabbi from Nazareth. Have you heard talk of Him?"

She received another shake of the head.

"He came to Capernaum several years ago, and He taught in synagogues all over the region. He performed many miracles, healing the sick and the lame and the blind. Even lepers were made clean. I saw Him heal a young man who was mute since birth. I knew Hevel. I knew he couldn't speak. But after Yeshua touched him, he spoke to me."

"You saw all of this for yourself?" Anah's eyes were wide.

"Yes. And more." She pictured Bilhah, the woman that she had been and the woman she had become after her encounter with Yeshua.

Anah had done Zlata a favor. But would she continue to do so if she knew the whole truth? Zlata decided to take the risk. "My master, Taneli, does not wish for me to follow the rabbi, to listen to His teaching. He has forbidden it. But I…I need to see Yeshua while I can. I don't think He will return to Galilee, so this week may be my last chance."

"I won't betray you."

"The punishment would be great if he found out." Zlata swallowed. "Perhaps for you, as well as for me."

Anah sat up straighter. "I won't betray you."

CHAPTER TWENTY-NINE

The next day, Zlata left Barukh's house in midmorning. Anticipation quickened her steps. Where might she find Yeshua in this vast city? Would He be in the temple? Would He be teaching in one of the many synagogues spread throughout Jerusalem? Or would He be outside the gates, the way He'd so often been outside Capernaum and other towns and villages?

Anah followed behind Zlata at a safe distance, pretending to shadow her steps in case Taneli had paid someone in addition to the young slave girl to watch her. Zlata was deep into the city before the pair of them dropped the ruse and began walking side by side. By that time, Zlata had looked at dozens of pots, many mats, and several fine examples of dyed cloth.

They were a few streets away from the Temple Mount, passing by the wares of a carpenter, when Zlata overheard someone speak the name Yeshua. She stopped and looked around. Her heart nearly stopped when she saw three Pharisees, almost within arm's length from where she stood. How foolish of her. Taneli could be anywhere in the city, and it was likely he was either in the temple or somewhere nearby. He wasn't with these three, but he could have been. And if he should see her…

She drew her scarf forward and dipped her head as she turned her back toward them. However, she didn't move away. She wanted to hear what they had to say about Yeshua.

"It was outrageous," one of the Pharisees said, either unaware that passersby could hear him or not caring. "He drove out everyone who was buying and selling in the temple. He overturned the tables of the moneychangers and the seats of those who were selling doves. He said they had turned a house of prayer into a robbers' den."

Another spoke up, his tone indignant. "There were children crying, 'Hosanna to the Son of David.' You heard it. As if He was more than a carpenter."

"But what about the healings?" the third man asked. "There were the blind and the lame who came to Him, and He healed them. Right there in the temple."

"They were *paid*, Mikhah. They *pretended* to be blind and lame. The people are easily manipulated."

"I'm not so sure."

When was this? Zlata longed to ask them. *Did it just happen? Is Yeshua even now in the temple?*

As if in answer, one of the Pharisees said, "It shouldn't trouble us. He went back to Bethany last night and hasn't been seen in the city today. Perhaps He'll think twice before trying to do anything like that again."

"The chief priests wanted to seize Him right then, but the people were too many. They believe Him to be a prophet, and they protect Him."

He is more than a prophet. He is the Anointed One, sent by God.

"Don't worry. They will find a way. He won't continue to escape them. If the chief priests can't trap Him any other way, they'll see that the Romans take Him in hand."

Tears blurred Zlata's vision as she walked away from the three Pharisees. Romans. The chief priests would turn the Romans on Yeshua. Surely not. Surely the religious leaders wouldn't do such a thing to one of their own people.

"What is it?" Anah asked in a hushed voice. "What's wrong?"

"Let us go back. I've seen enough for today."

"Tell me what's wrong."

Zlata shook her head.

"But I thought you wanted to find that rabbi you spoke of. That Yeshua."

"I do. But I overheard that He went to stay in Bethany last night. He isn't in the city today."

"How can you be sure?"

"I can't be sure," Zlata answered. "But I've been away long enough. And you will need to report to Taneli when he returns."

"Is that why you're sad?"

"No." Zlata glanced over her shoulder toward the temple. "No, I'm sad because there are so many who want to destroy Yeshua. He's in terrible danger, and there is nothing I can do to help Him."

"No, there is nothing. You are only a woman."

Zlata stopped abruptly and looked at the girl. "We are wrong. We are both wrong. I can pray for Yeshua. I *must* pray for Him. Even a woman's prayers count for something." She turned to face the Temple Mount. "And tomorrow I will go to the temple to pray."

Zlata did pray for Yeshua that day. She prayed for His safety over and over again. With nothing to do but sit idly, she found herself a shaded corner in the garden and prayed in every way she'd been taught. She continued to pray, even as the afternoon warmth began to make her drowsy.

It was there that Anah found her. "You are wanted," the girl said, placing a hand on Zlata's shoulder.

"Taneli has sent for me?" She stood, uncertain what the summons might mean. A shiver shot through her as a possibility sprang to mind.

"No. Not your master. It is someone else. A woman. She awaits you near the stables. I will show you."

"But I don't know anyone in Jerusalem."

Zlata followed Anah along a narrow, well-groomed path to where Barukh kept his horses. A man was working with one of the beautiful gold-colored animals in an open area. The horse reared up, striking the air with its hooves, and Zlata stopped in her tracks. She had always been fond of donkeys with their big ears and docile manner. The horse before her was another matter. It frightened her, perhaps because in Israel only the very wealthy and the Romans owned such mighty steeds.

"Zlata." The voice came from the shadows cast by a row of trees.

She turned quickly in response. "Bilhah?" She couldn't believe it. In a city of this size…after so long a time…a friend… her friend.

"It is I." Bilhah stepped into the sunlight.

She forgot to be afraid. She didn't care if she was seen. She embraced Bilhah. "How did you find me?" she whispered. "How did you know I was here?"

"Taneli was seen in the synagogue on the temple grounds. We inquired where he was staying while in Jerusalem."

"*He* told you."

"No." Bilhah laughed softly. "Someone else told us."

"You are still with Yeshua."

"Yes." There was a tenderness in Bilhah's smile that tugged at Zlata's heart.

"I was praying for His safety when Anah came for me just now."

Bilhah's smile faded. "Not long ago, Yeshua took the twelve aside and told them that we were all going up to Jerusalem. He said the Son of Man will be delivered to the chief priests and the scribes. He said they will condemn Him to death and will hand Him over to the Gentiles. They will mock Him and spit on Him. They will scourge and kill Him."

Zlata sucked in a breath. Covering her mouth with her hand, she whispered, "Tell me it isn't so."

"It's what He said will happen. But He also said that three days later He will rise again."

Impossible, Zlata thought. But immediately guilt squeezed her heart. How could she think anything was impossible if the Messiah said it was so? Still, she would rather pray that He would be delivered from the danger at hand, that He would never be condemned to death or mocked or scourged or killed.

She would keep praying for His deliverance. Yeshua Himself had told stories about the importance of persistent prayer. She would practice it now.

"I had better go," Bilhah said, intruding on Zlata's troubled thoughts. "But Yeshua said we are going to the temple tomorrow. Will you look for us there?"

"Yes. Yes, I will be there. I will look for you tomorrow."

CHAPTER THIRTY

Zlata slept little that night. She heard every sigh, every snore, every turning on a cot from the other female servants in the small room. She heard some of them rise well before dawn so they could begin preparing food for the household. She heard others leave the quarters soon after for their own appointed duties.

When it was Anah's turn, she leaned over Zlata's mat and whispered, "I am to follow you again today. If your master stays with us long enough, I shall be rich."

At another time, Zlata might have laughed. A slave did not grow rich on one small copper coin a day. But then she realized Anah already possessed as much money as Zlata herself. Two mites. And after today, Anah would, indeed, be the richer of the two.

Zlata was the last to rise from her mat, the last to wash with water poured into a small clay basin, the last to brush her hair before covering it with a white headscarf. After breaking her fast, she waited to know if she might be summoned by either Taneli or Abra. She didn't expect it, especially since Anah had already been instructed to follow Zlata for a third day. Still she waited until the slave girl came to inform her that Taneli had left the villa. Only then did she venture out.

As they had done the previous day, Zlata went out alone and Anah followed some distance behind. But today, once away from the homes of the wealthy in the Upper City, Zlata didn't pretend to look at merchandise in the various stalls she passed. She had one destination in mind, and nothing would detain her from reaching it.

A pall of smoke from the animal sacrifices hung over the temple, and the noise of venders hawking their wares grew louder the closer Zlata got to the southern wall of the mount. Anah had caught up with her by then, and the girl now gripped Zlata's arm, determined not to get separated. The crowd jostled the two women this way and that, scarcely paying them any mind at all. How, Zlata wondered, did Taneli avoid touching a woman—something he never wanted to do on a public thoroughfare—in a mass of people such as this?

Zlata led Anah into the place where they could be ritually cleansed, along with other pilgrims, before entering the temple precincts. Afterward, they climbed the steps toward the Double Gate. Even though Zlata had been there once before, she was still filled with awe. Long ago, she had overheard Taneli say that the Temple Mount—as modified by Herod the Great—took up one-sixth of the city. The sheer size of everything overwhelmed her. It seemed to frighten Anah, who held on even tighter than before.

Zlata and Anah were crossing the Court of the Gentiles when Zlata caught sight of Bilhah. Her friend stood near the *soreg*. Beyond the latticed screen lay the temple courts, off limits to the gentiles. Bilhah saw Zlata and smiled.

"I've been watching for you," she said as Zlata and Anah drew close. "Anah, it is good to see you again."

"And you, my lady," Anah returned shyly, her gaze lowered in respect.

A strange look filled Bilhah's eyes.

Perhaps, Zlata thought, her friend remembered it wasn't so long ago that she'd been addressed by very different names and with much less respect.

Then a smile returned to Bilhah's mouth and she said, "Yeshua is in the Court of Women even now. Come. Let us join Him."

Anah drew back. "I should wait for you outside."

"No, Anah. You are not unclean. Come with me. I want you to hear the rabbi for yourself."

The girl allowed herself to be drawn forward.

The three women traversed the courtyard around the corner to the Eastern Gate of the temple. Once through the massive doorways, they climbed the steps to the balconies above the colonnades and looked down upon the many pilgrims filling the court. There looked to be thousands of people, both men and women. Many dropped offerings into one of the trumpet-shaped boxes. Others stood in groups, talking. Some men pressed on toward the Nicanor Gate, where they could observe the temple sacrifices.

"There," Bilhah said, excitement in her voice. "There is Yeshua." She pointed.

The rabbi was almost beneath them.

Zlata held her breath and stared down into the court. Unexpectedly, Yeshua looked up toward the women standing in the balcony. His gaze found Zlata and He smiled, as if He knew her, before turning toward a number of Pharisees who had approached Him and His disciples.

"Teacher," one of them said, "we know that You are truthful and defer to no one; for You are not partial to any, but teach the way of God in truth."

One of the other Pharisees turned slightly, and Zlata's breath stopped in her chest. *Taneli.* She drew slightly back from the edge of the balcony.

"Is it lawful to pay a poll-tax to Caesar, or not?" the first Pharisee asked. "Shall we pay or shall we not pay?"

Zlata understood they were trying to trap Yeshua. She had listened to Taneli's plans to do just that many times.

Yeshua seemed unruffled by the questions. "Why are you testing Me? Bring Me a denarius to look at."

Someone handed Him the coin.

"Whose likeness and inscription is this?" He held the denarius in His open palm.

"Caesar's," came the answer from several men.

Yeshua said, "Render to Caesar the things that are Caesar's, and to God the things that are God's."

Some Sadducees pressed in and began questioning Him, but Zlata had ceased to listen. For some reason, her thoughts had traveled back to that morning, to when she'd realized that after this day, even a slave girl in Barukh's household would have more money than she possessed.

Zlata had held on to two mites for ten years. At first, it was because Yerik had given them to her. The coins and the blue scarf she'd wrapped them in were part of her treasured memories. And she'd kept the coins because she had nothing else but the clothes on her back. She'd been afraid to let go, afraid of the future, afraid of being in want.

Her glance flicked to Taneli, who had moved off with his fellow Pharisees.

Afraid. I'm tired of being afraid. Adonai, help me.

An argument broke out below her and she leaned forward again.

A man who looked to be a scribe said, "Rabbi, what commandment is the foremost of all?"

Zlata's heart seemed to answer right along with Yeshua.

"Hear, O Israel! The Lord our God is one Lord; and you shall love the Lord your God with all your heart, and with all your soul, and with all your mind, and with all your strength." Yeshua swept his gaze over the men crowded around him, His voice growing stronger. "The second is this, 'You shall love your neighbor as yourself.' There is no other commandment greater than these."

"And you shall love the Lord your God with all your heart, and with all your soul, and with all your mind, and with all your strength." The words echoed not only in Zlata's mind but in her soul. *Have I loved God with all that I am? Have I?*

The scribe must have said something more to Yeshua, for He said to him, "You are not far from the kingdom of God."

After that, the Sadducees moved away from Him. Perhaps they were afraid to ask more questions that would simply prove

Yeshua knew the scriptures in a way they did not. But Yeshua didn't need their questions. He went on teaching the crowd that had gathered around Him.

Zlata saw her father-in-law again. He and the other Pharisees stood within listening distance of the rabbi, Taneli's face scrunched in a thunderous frown.

As if feeling the look, Yeshua turned toward Taneli and said, "Beware of the scribes who like to walk around in long robes, and like respectful greetings in the market places, and chief seats in the synagogues and places of honor at banquets, who devour widows' houses, and for appearance's sake offer long prayers; these will receive greater condemnation."

Zlata's breath caught again, for she could see in Taneli's face that Yeshua's words had found their mark. An angry murmur rose from the group of religious leaders. And as the sound filled her ears, she knew what she wanted to do. She knew what she *needed* to do. She needed to give everything to God. Because of Yeshua. Because of the Messiah. Because His words held light and life for all who would listen. Despite her fears, she wanted to give everything she was and everything she had.

She reached into the small sack tucked within the folds of her tunic. A moment later, she withdrew the two copper coins. She stared at them in the palm of her hand.

"Render to Caesar the things that are Caesar's, and to God the things that are God's."

Her fingers closed tightly around the copper coins. Two mites. That was all. It was an insignificant amount of money, but it was everything she had. She moved toward the steps that would take her down to the Court of Women.

The nearest offering box was not far from where Yeshua now sat, several of His men nearby. But Yeshua wasn't talking to them nor was He teaching. Instead His gaze was on the people all around Him. Zlata glanced His way then back toward the colonnade. She slowed her steps, waiting for other people—much richer people—to put their offerings into the box. The sound of dropping coins seemed to echo all around her. Purses emptying coins upon coins.

She had only a few steps left to go when she saw Taneli step into her line of vision. The thunder was back in his eyes. He knew she'd come to the temple to see and hear Yeshua. He knew she'd defied him. For a moment, she expected him to reach out, grab her by the hair, and strike her again and again. Terror sluiced through her and her legs felt weak. Even so, she took another step forward.

A song of praise rose unexpectedly within her. *Praise the* Lord! *Praise God in His sanctuary; praise Him in His mighty expanse. Praise Him for His mighty deeds; praise Him according to His excellent greatness.*

She took the final two steps to the offering box, held out her hand, and dropped the two mites. Fear mingled with a sense of freedom as they clinked against other coins.

She glanced up and saw the hatred in Taneli's eyes. The look said she would pay for this moment. She would pay dearly.

Then she turned, and this time she found Yeshua looking at her. He didn't smile, and yet it seemed almost like He did.

His eyes promised something quite different than Taneli's. His eyes were full of love and compassion. It stirred hope in her heart. After a few moments, He looked to His men and spoke to them in a voice she could not hear.

Strength returned to her shaky legs, and lifting her chin, Zlata walked toward the balcony staircase where Anah awaited her.

CHAPTER THIRTY-ONE

On still quivering legs, Zlata walked with Anah until they reached the street beyond the Temple Mount.

"Will you be all right?" she asked the girl. "When you return to your master's house without me, will you be punished?"

"No. Barukh won't punish me. I will be all right. Although I don't think your master will give me the coin he promised for following you today."

"No." Zlata gave her a wry smile. "I don't suppose he will."

Anah lowered her eyes for a few moments then looked up again. "May God bless you, Zlata."

"And you, Anah. Thank you for your kindness to me."

"I will remember you and all that you told me. I will remember the rabbi and what He said today."

Zlata took a step back, and with a small wave of goodbye, Anah turned and disappeared into the crowd of people pressing into the city.

Before she could wonder what to do next, she heard Bilhah ask, "Are you ready? We should be on our way."

Zlata turned around. She hadn't known her friend had followed them out of the temple, although now that she saw her, she wasn't surprised. "Where are we going?"

"To Bethany."

"To Bethany? To where Yeshua is staying?"

Bilhah nodded.

Zlata had known, in the moment she'd dropped her two coins into the offering box, that she had no place to go. She'd known that, should she return to Barukh's house, Taneli would punish her as he'd not punished her before. She'd known she couldn't return to Capernaum. She was without family or resources and alone in a big city with no way to support herself. The realization had been part of her terror, although it hadn't stopped her from doing what she'd felt compelled to do. She'd needed to give all she had to God, and so she had. And with it she had given away any remnants of security she'd possessed.

But now, there was Bilhah, showing her that the Lord God had already made provision for her. Zlata began to weep, hiding her face in her hands.

"Come." Her friend's arm went around her shoulders. "I'll show you the way."

To Zlata, the words had a double meaning.

They moved against the stream of Jewish pilgrims who were pressing into Jerusalem for the Passover, now only two days away. After passing through the city gates, they followed the road toward Jericho, crossing the Kidron Valley.

"It isn't far to Bethany," Bilhah said. "We're staying at the home of Lazarus. You will like his sisters, Mary and Martha. They have shown me great kindness. They will make you welcome too."

"Lazarus. Isn't he the friend of Yeshua who died and was raised to life?"

"Yes."

"Taneli tried to make certain I heard nothing about Yeshua after all of you left Galilee, but he couldn't keep me from hearing of that. Women still talk when they gather at the well."

Bilhah laughed softly. "Yes, they always talk when at the well."

"Were you there that day? At the tomb?"

"I was there. I saw Lazarus walk out, still wrapped in his grave clothes. He had to be set free from the cloths that bound him."

A shiver ran through Zlata. To see a dead man, four days in the tomb, rise again, walking, still bound…

"There are some who want to kill Lazarus, almost as much as they want to kill the Master. They talk about it openly."

"I'm afraid for Yeshua," Zlata said, her pulse quickening. "He should go away. He should go far from here until the danger passes. Perhaps as far as Egypt."

Bilhah looked at Zlata but said nothing. Her eyes held an emotion Zlata couldn't define. Did her old friend agree with her or not? Was she afraid for Yeshua too? Zlata couldn't tell.

"He won't go, will He?"

"No," Bilhah answered. "He won't go. Yeshua set His face toward Jerusalem long ago. He goes where His Father sends Him. Now, that is the holy city."

They walked the remainder of the way to Bethany in silence.

Bilhah was right. Zlata did like Lazarus's two sisters. Mary and Martha welcomed her into their home as if she were a long-lost relative. It wasn't uncommon, of course, for Jews to extend warm hospitality to friends and strangers alike. It was almost second nature, even to the poorest among them. From the time they were children, faithful Jews were trained to be hospitable.

The household was busy making preparations for a banquet that night, to be held at the nearby home of a man known as Simon the leper. It was Martha who explained to Zlata that Simon had been healed of the dreaded disease by Yeshua, but the name still clung to him.

"I believe he wears it proudly," Martha added, "because it allows him to tell again and again the story of how he was healed. Being called Simon the leper allows him to thank Yeshua, the Son of God, and to praise Adonai over and over."

Zlata made herself useful, helping in the preparation of the meal. Martha kept an eye on everything—the roasting meat, the simmering stew, the fresh vegetables and fruit, the loaves of bread. She made certain there was an adequate amount of wine to serve all the guests who'd been invited.

It was late in the afternoon when Yeshua and His followers returned to Bethany. While the men remained in the courtyard with the rabbi, several more women joined in the meal preparations. After introductions were made, one of the women, another named Mary who was from Magdala, shared what had transpired after Yeshua left the temple.

"We were all sitting on the Mount of Olives, opposite the Temple Mount, and Yeshua said that not one stone of the temple will be left upon another. It will all be torn down."

Zlata's gasp joined with several others. How could that be?

"And several of His disciples who were nearest to Him asked when that would happen. He answered them, starting with a warning not to let anyone mislead them. He spoke of wars and rumors of war. He spoke of one nation rising against another. He said His disciples will be delivered to the courts and flogged in the synagogues and some will stand before governors and kings for His sake, as a testimony. He said we will all be hated because of His name."

Mary continued to talk, but Zlata had ceased to listen. Icy tentacles of fear had gripped her heart and made her deaf at the same time. She recalled Taneli's rages. She pictured him with a stick in his hand, ready to whip the flesh off her back for choosing to follow Yeshua. In her mind, the images of war and death and flogging and hatred were all too real. So real she could almost reach out and touch those who suffered.

A hand upon her shoulder brought Zlata back to the kitchen. She glanced to see Bilhah standing next to her, her gaze intent upon Mary.

"And He said they will see the Son of Man coming in clouds with great power and glory, and He will send angels to gather up His elect from the four winds. He ended with a warning for us to be on the alert for all of these things."

When Mary stopped speaking, the room fell silent, save for the soft bubbling sounds of a simmering stew.

As Zlata entered the house of Simon the leper that night, she couldn't help but remember a different supper in the home of another man named Simon. Two years ago, she had been present only to serve the men who reclined at table. She had been a woman of no importance, a servant, lost in the shadows. Tonight, she was an invited guest.

Oil lamps provided illumination along the walls and in the corners. Yeshua was given the place of honor at the head of the table farthest from the courtyard. Zlata and Bilhah were seated at the table to the right of the doorway. Delicious odors wafted on the air, causing Zlata's stomach to rumble with hunger.

Over a meal of roasted meats, bread and vegetables dipped in olive oil, fresh fruits, and a hearty stew, Zlata listened to story after story of Yeshua as He'd ministered in the towns of Judea and Perea over the past year. Someone recounted His parable of the Good Shepherd. Someone else shared His story of the Good Samaritan. Bilhah shared another lesson the rabbi had taught about prayer.

Like bread soaking up the liquid in a stew, Zlata soaked in the words she heard, not quite believing that she was in this house, with these women, within earshot of Yeshua. The joy that bubbled up inside of her made it easy to forget the dangers that surrounded her Lord. How could anything bad befall the Son of God? He was the Messiah, the coming King.

As the evening progressed, Zlata grew sleepy. She wasn't used to so much good food and wine. She feared she might embarrass herself by falling asleep at the table.

Then Mary, the sister of Lazarus, rose from her place at the table and made her way across the room to where Yeshua reclined at table. In her hands she carried an alabaster vial. Sleep was forgotten as Zlata watched Mary break the narrow neck of the vial. Then she poured the contents onto Yeshua's head. Even from where Zlata sat, she could smell the wonderful fragrance of the perfume.

A disciple at a nearby table said to his neighbor, "Why this waste? For this perfume might have been sold for a high price and the money given to the poor."

Yeshua looked around the room, love and patience in His eyes as His gaze moved from table to table, from person to person. At last He said, "Why do you bother the woman? For she has done a good deed to Me." His gaze went to the disciple who'd spoken the question to his neighbor. "For you always have the poor with you; but you do not always have Me. For when she poured this perfume on My body, she did it to prepare Me for burial."

Tears sprang to Zlata's eyes, and her breath caught in her chest.

"Truly I say to you, wherever this gospel is preached in the whole world, what this woman has done will also be spoken of in memory of her."

Lord, I have no costly perfume to pour out for You. But may I have the same extravagant love for You so that I pour myself out for Your good news for the remainder of my life.

As if He'd heard the silent prayer, Yeshua looked across the room at Zlata. Like before, she believed He saw not only her face but into her heart. She hoped what He found there was pleasing to Him.

CHAPTER THIRTY-TWO

Bilhah and Zlata remained in Bethany to help Martha and Mary with preparations for the Passover meal. Yeshua and His closest disciples returned to Jerusalem, making the home of Lazarus seem unusually quiet with their absence.

Close to midday, Zlata went to refill a water jar at the well. She was just about to heft it to her shoulder for the short walk back to the house when a familiar voice spoke her name. Sucking in a breath, not daring to hope she'd heard correctly, she turned.

Joel stood in the street, his head covered by a multicolored scarf, a band of braided fabric securing it in place. He'd gained muscle over the past year. How strong he looked.

"I was told Yeshua was staying at the home of His friend Lazarus," he said, a gentle smile on his lips. "I hoped to see Bilhah when I got here. I couldn't believe it when she told me you were here too."

Zlata's heart beat rapidly. "I didn't think I would ever see you again. It's been so long."

He nodded. "Too long."

"I was…I was sorry when I learned Taneli turned you out of the vineyard."

"You couldn't have been surprised."

She swallowed hard. "I wasn't surprised. But I was sorry. It was my fault. I never should have asked you to—"

"You're wrong. It wasn't your fault. I knew Taneli would disapprove. I knew you'd been forbidden to seek out Yeshua." He took a step closer to her. "I tried to see you after that day. Were you told?"

Her chest tightened. Tightened until it hurt. "No."

"I waited in Capernaum for several days, hoping I would see you going to the well or to the market. You never came."

She hadn't been able to leave her sleeping mat for two weeks, her body too bruised and battered to move at first. She lowered her eyes rather than tell him that.

"But here you are, Zlata. And you look well."

Still without anything to say, she lifted the water jar so she could begin the walk back to the house.

"I've been invited to stay for Passover," he said.

She smiled as he fell into step beside her, a respectful distance between them.

As Zlata had seen him do in the past, Joel walked with his arms behind his back, one hand holding the wrist of the other. "Bilhah told me what happened at the temple. It was brave of you."

"Brave?" She glanced at him. "No. I...I was terrified. But I had to do it."

"It's brave to do what you must, to do what is right, even when you're afraid."

"I am always afraid," she whispered.

Joel didn't reply, and she hoped he hadn't heard her.

"Where have you been all this time?" she asked after another short silence.

"I couldn't find work in Galilee. Taneli's influence carries weight throughout the region. But I'm now the steward for a vineyard in Judea. To the south of Jerusalem." He motioned in the general direction. "The owner, Matthias, is a good and just man, and he pays his workers a fair wage. Like us, he has come to believe that Yeshua is the Messiah."

She smiled as she looked at Joel. "Because of you?"

"No." He returned the smile. "Because of Yeshua. But I had something to do with my master listening to Him teach."

They arrived at Lazarus's home, and Joel lifted the latch on the courtyard door, holding it open for Zlata to pass through.

Bilhah, who stood near the cookstove, smiled when she saw them. "Good. You found her."

Embarrassed for some reason, Zlata's cheeks grew warm. "I must take the water in," she said without glancing at Joel, then she hurried away.

She set the large jar in its usual spot then looked to see if there was something else she needed to do. But Mary made a shooing motion. "Go outside. Sit in the shade and rest. Everything is well in hand. Yeshua and His men are eating Passover in the city tonight. We will be only a few."

"Yeshua isn't eating Passover here?"

"No."

Joel will be disappointed that he's missed Him.

She turned on her heel and went to the doorway. Joel had settled onto a bench in the shade of a tree. His head was leaned back against the bark, and his eyes were closed. Behind him in a pen, a donkey munched on hay while a goat drank water from a nearby trough.

"Here," Mary said. "Give him these dates. He is probably hungry. Men usually are."

Zlata accepted the fruit, holding them in hands cupped together. She went outside and approached Joel. She was as silent as could be, but he must have heard her anyway, for his eyes opened and he straightened away from the tree at once.

"Mary thought you might be hungry." Zlata held out her hands toward him.

"I am." He grinned, looking almost boyish in his enthusiasm for the offered food. Then he cupped his own hands and let her drop the dates into them. "Join me," he said before she could move away.

Zlata glanced toward the house, as if expecting someone to forbid such a thing. Taneli would never have allowed a woman to sit with a man in the courtyard to simply pass the time of day. It was considered unacceptable behavior by many. Most certainly by the Pharisees.

"Yeshua often talks with women," Joel said, as if reading her mind. "Even strangers. He includes them as disciples and teaches them His truths. Does He not?"

"He does."

"Then sit and talk with me as I fill my belly with dates."

She was unable to resist. She sat on the opposite end of the short bench.

Joel popped a date into his mouth, chewed, and swallowed. After a moment, he said, "Did I tell you I have a house of my own on the edge of the vineyard?" He picked up another date and rolled it gently between thumb and forefinger. "It's larger than Keziah's house. Not much but some. It has a small court-yard on the north side and stairs leading up to the roof."

"I'm glad for you."

"A man could raise a family there."

A rushing sound filled Zlata's ears as she lowered her gaze to her hands, now folded in her lap. She recalled Dara saying… something…something to do with Joel.

"We have known each other for many years, Zlata. You came to the vineyard with Yerik several times."

She gave her head the slightest shake.

"I saw how you loved your husband. I saw how you honored him. How you mourned him."

"You couldn't have seen so much. Our paths haven't crossed that often."

"Often enough. I know what I observed."

"What—" She swallowed then looked up. "What are you saying, Joel?"

"I'm saying I want to marry you, Zlata. I want you to walk with me through this life. I want to honor you and protect you." His voice softened. "I want to give you children who will be a blessing to us both in our old age."

It took effort to draw a breath. She didn't know how to respond, what to say. Her father had arranged her marriage to Yerik. Although he'd chosen well for her, he had done the choosing.

When Yerik died, Zlata's life had fallen under the care and direction of Taneli. Rarely had she made any decision without the oversight of a man. How could she know what was right to do now that she was completely on her own? What if she chose wrong? What if Joel wasn't all that he appeared to be? What if, as a husband, he was more like Taneli than Yerik? What if—

"Zlata, I believe we could love each other."

Staring into his eyes, she remembered that he had never shown her anything but kindness. Even when she disliked him, he had been kind. And he believed in Yeshua, as she did. He couldn't be like Taneli.

"Think on it," he said.

Head bowed, she rose from the bench. "I will, Joel. I will think on it." Then she hurried inside.

"You are troubled, my friend," Bilhah whispered that night, long after the end of the Passover meal.

Zlata rolled onto her side on the sleeping mat. The room was pitch dark, but still she stared in Bilhah's direction.

"Would you tell me what it is?" her friend asked.

"Joel," she whispered in return.

"Ah. I thought as much."

"He has…he has asked me to marry him."

"And your answer?"

Zlata chewed her lower lip for a moment. "I haven't given him one yet."

"Why not?" Bilhah's voice rose above a whisper, threatening to wake the other women asleep in the same room.

Because I'm afraid. "What if it isn't what God wants for me?"

"A husband who would love and cherish you. Why would God deny you that?"

"I could not follow Yeshua if I were to marry. Joel works on a vineyard. He is tied to the land. I would not be free, as you are, to go wherever Yeshua goes."

Bilhah's hand fell upon Zlata's shoulder. "I have learned this past year that there are many ways to follow Yeshua. The first and most important way is with your heart."

Zlata closed her eyes against the welling tears, but she couldn't stop them from falling and dampening the cushion beneath her head.

I'm afraid, Adonai. I don't know what to do. How does a person discern Your will? What if I make the wrong choice?

She imagined herself sitting at Yeshua's feet, listening to Him, learning from Him. But she could also imagine herself walking beside Joel.

Help me know what to do. The words repeated over and over in her mind until she finally drifted off to sleep.

CHAPTER THIRTY-THREE

It was early the next morning, as Zlata worked at the mill, grinding wheat for that day's bread, when a boy stumbled into the courtyard. He looked to be about twelve or thirteen years old. His face was sweaty, and he panted for breath, as if he'd run a great distance.

"Is this the home of Lazarus?" he asked, his voice cracking.

Martha answered from the doorway. "Yes. He is inside." She motioned for the boy to enter.

Zlata rose from the mill, her heart racing as if she was the one who'd been running. Almost reluctantly, she moved toward the doorway. She saw Martha, a hand over her mouth. Then she saw Mary step to Martha's side, their arms going around each other.

"The chief priests were delivering Him to the governor," the boy said. "That's when I was told to come for you."

Lazarus looked up, his gaze going to his sisters. "He warned us, but still I didn't believe Him."

Unnoticed, Zlata slipped inside and went to the water jar. She filled a cup and carried it to the boy. She didn't fully understand what news he'd brought with him, but she knew it was bad.

"Let's begin again," Lazarus said, his gaze returning to the boy. "First, what is your name?"

"I am Reuel, son of John."

"Reuel, start over. You said Yeshua was arrested in the Garden of Gethsemane?"

Arrested? Zlata pressed a hand to the base of her throat.

The boy drained the cup then set it on the table. "Yes. I saw them leaving the house where they must have eaten the Passover meal. I recognized Yeshua. I saw Him come into the city when everyone was shouting and cheering. I followed them."

He looked like a crafty boy of the streets, Zlata thought. Perhaps he'd followed the group of men so he might try to steal a purse or two.

"I've heard many stories about the rabbi. I wanted to see what He would do. I wanted to see a miracle. But all Yeshua did was go off to pray. The others with Him fell asleep." He glanced around the room. "I fell asleep too. I was wakened by the sound of marching and metal. There was a great crowd of men, some carrying torches, others carrying swords and clubs."

Mary cried out with alarm.

"They took Him and led Him to the high priest." Reuel spoke with more excitement now, as if he'd warmed to the story. "I couldn't go into the courtyard, but I could see in. There were many others there, milling about, sitting by fires to keep warm, waiting. Someone in the street said the entire council was inside with…with Caiaphas. I sat down and waited, just like those inside the courtyard, but I fell asleep again. When I awoke, it was dawn. That's when I saw them leading Yeshua out. He was bound at the wrists. Someone came up to me. I don't know who it was. One of His disciples, I think. I don't know why he trusted me either. Maybe he saw me in the garden. He gave me a coin and told me to run here with the news. So I did."

Lazarus stood. "We must go into the city at once." He reached into his purse, withdrew a coin, and handed it to the boy. "Thank you for fulfilling your mission, Reuel. May God bless you for it."

"You don't—"

"Keep it," Lazarus interrupted. "You have done us a service."

Within minutes, they were on the road, headed for Jerusalem—everyone who had stayed at Lazarus's home the previous night, as well as those who had spent the night at the home of Simon the leper, Joel among them. Lazarus set a brisk pace, and no one seemed inclined to want to waste breath talking.

This can't be happening. It can't be.

Those words repeated themselves over and over in Zlata's head as she walked. But even as she tried to convince herself, she remembered what Bilhah had told her only a few days before. That Yeshua had taken His closest disciples aside and warned them that He would be delivered to the chief priests, that He would be condemned to death, that He would be scourged and killed.

He must be mistaken. That can't happen to Yeshua. He is the Messiah. It cannot happen.

It seemed that the entire world had poured into Jerusalem for the Passover. Zlata was grateful when Joel took hold of her arm, steadying her as they followed Lazarus and the others across the city toward Herod's Palace, Pilate's official headquarters.

Adonai, have mercy. Adonai, don't let Yeshua be harmed. Almighty God, protect Him by Your mighty hand.

As they drew closer to the palace, the mood of the crowd around them seemed to change, darken even. Fear wound around Zlata's heart and tried to squeeze the life from her. She stumbled, but Joel's grip on her arm steadied her again.

Outside of the palace—within the Praetorium itself—was a raised stone pavement used for official announcements and judgments. Despite the masses pressing in to see for themselves what was happening, Lazarus and his party managed to get within sight of that stone in time to see Yeshua, the Messiah, being led away.

"Crucify Him!" A shout went up near Zlata.

"No!" she cried in response. "No!"

Zlata wept as they walked behind Yeshua, two other convicted men, Roman guards, many priests and scribes, and a throng of spectators. Followers of Yeshua were among them, but so were the curious and the hecklers. The march to Golgotha, located beyond the Gennath Gate, seemed to take an eternity, but in reality it was not even midmorning.

When they arrived at the place where the three men were to be crucified—a place easily seen from the public road, a warning to passersby of the might of Rome—Joel guided Zlata through those who had gathered to watch. It took a while before she realized that they stood near Mary the mother of Yeshua, John the son of Zebedee, Mary of Magdala, and Bilhah. The sound of weeping filled her ears, and through a blur of her own tears, she watched as they stripped Yeshua of His garments, drove stakes into His hands and feet, and hoisted His cross into place between the two other men condemned to death. A sign was posted above Yeshua that read THE KING OF THE JEWS.

Someone on the road shouted, "Ha! You who are going to destroy the temple and rebuild it in three days, save Yourself, and come down from the cross!"

Joel stiffened, and for a moment, Zlata thought he would bolt for the road and strike whoever had hurled the abuse. But instead, his arm went around Zlata's waist.

Then she heard a dreaded but familiar voice. "He saved others; He cannot save Himself!"

She turned her head, searching the crowd, until she found the cluster of Pharisees, watching from a distance. Taneli was there, his expression one of triumph and hatred.

"Let this Messiah, this King of Israel, now come down from the cross," her father-in-law continued, "so that we may see and believe!"

Softly, Zlata replied, "You don't know what you say. You don't know who He is. You are blind, Taneli. You are so very blind."

Then she heard Yeshua speak from the cross, saying, "Father, forgive them, for they do not know what they are doing."

Even now. Even now You forgive. I cannot forgive, but You do. Even here. Even now.

Time passed, but it seemed more wretchedly slow than the walk to this Place of a Skull had been.

At the sixth hour, when the sun was directly overhead, darkness suddenly fell over the earth. Zlata looked up, expecting to find storm clouds gathered, but there was no impending storm. There were no clouds. Only the darkness of night in the midst of the day. Many were frightened by the strangeness and left Golgotha, hurrying back into the city or to their villages and campsites. Zlata wondered if Taneli had left as well. Would he linger when even the heavens told him he'd made a mistake? But she didn't look. It would be useless in the dark, and he wasn't her concern.

Adonai, have mercy. He is surely Your Son. I don't understand how You can let this happen to Him.

An hour passed in the darkness, then another, and another. Zlata leaned into Joel throughout, sometimes weeping against him, sometimes listening as others wept nearby. Neither of them spoke. What was it they could say when the incomprehensible happened before their eyes?

When the darkness lifted, as suddenly as it had fallen, Zlata straightened, looking up at the blue of the afternoon sky.

Then she heard the Messiah cry out in a loud voice, "My God, My God, why have You forsaken Me?"

Zlata's heart seemed to rip in two as she looked toward the cross again.

"Father, into Your hands I commit My spirit."

By the way His head lolled to one side, Zlata knew He had breathed His last. Mary, His mother, fell to her knees, wailing. John held her by the shoulders as she cried. Others began to mourn loudly as well. Men beat their chests. As if in response the earth shook beneath their feet. Joel's grasp tightened on Zlata as they both tried to keep their balance.

A centurion who stood not far from them said, "Certainly this man was innocent. Truly He was the Son of God!"

But it was too late for anyone in authority to declare Yeshua innocent. He was dead. There was no going back now.

CHAPTER THIRTY-FOUR

Once, Yeshua had said that He, the Son of Man, was Lord of the Sabbath. Zlata thought of that as she sat in Lazarus's courtyard the following day. She wasn't sure why, but the words wouldn't leave her alone. Perhaps because she longed to rise and return to Jerusalem, to go to the tomb that had been hastily provided for Yeshua by a wealthy man from Arimathea. She wanted to run there and sit and mourn Him openly. But she couldn't, for it was the Sabbath.

None of the twelve had returned to Bethany. Zlata had seen only John at the cross. What had happened to the others? Had they all fled? Had they been arrested? Were they in hiding? Should *she* be in hiding?

She recalled that look of hatred and triumph Taneli had worn on Golgotha, and fear coiled around her heart. He would rejoice if she was arrested and put to death. She didn't doubt it. And if the Messiah couldn't stop His own crucifixion, what hope had she of escaping the wrath of a powerful man should he choose to seek her out for punishment?

She rose and walked to the animal pen. Leaning on the top rail, she stared at the donkey inside. It stared back at her with doleful eyes. In her memory, she saw Yeshua riding another donkey toward the city gates, the people shouting,

"Hosanna! Hosanna!" as they spread cloaks and palm branches on the road before Him. Six days. How could so much have happened in only six days? From triumphal entry to crucifixion and a hasty burial in a borrowed tomb.

Tears welled up then trickled down her cheeks. She'd thought she would be out of tears by this time, but apparently there were more of them to be spent. Many more.

As she turned away from the pen, her gaze went to the house in time to see Bilhah stepping through the doorway. Zlata saw the sorrow on her friend's face and knew it mirrored her own.

"Should you eat something?" Bilhah asked.

"I'm not hungry."

Bilhah nodded as she crossed the courtyard. "I know." When she reached Zlata, she slipped her arm around her back, much as Joel had done the previous day, supporting her throughout the horrid ordeal.

Zlata pressed the side of her head against Bilhah's shoulder. "I can't bear it."

"I feel the same."

"I was in Bethany just two days. I sat down to supper with Him only once. If it is unbearable for me, how much worse it must be for you and the others who walked with Him and served Him for so long."

"Strange, but the amount of time spent with Yeshua didn't affect how any of us felt about Him. Knowing Yeshua, whether for a minute or a lifetime, was all it took for us to love Him."

"Not everyone felt that way."

"No." Bilhah sighed. "Not everyone. Some couldn't understand. Some were unwilling to see the truth. Some chose to hate instead of love."

Zlata raised her head. "He forgave them. Even from the cross, He forgave them for killing Him. He forgave those who hated Him."

"'Forgive us our debts,'" Bilhah whispered, "'as we also have forgiven our debtors.'"

It was as if Yeshua Himself whispered into her heart: *Forgive Taneli.*

She had known, ever since Bilhah had shared Yeshua's teaching on prayer more than a year before, that she needed to forgive her father-in-law. That Yeshua wanted that from her. She hadn't been able to do it. She'd resisted it every time she repeated the prayer He'd taught His disciples. And after Taneli had brutally punished her for seeking out the rabbi, she'd clung to her resentment even harder.

Forgive Taneli.

Bilhah drew her toward the bench, and they sat on it. "Did you ever hear Yeshua's story of the mustard seed?" she asked after a period of silence.

"No." Zlata's chest tightened, for she knew she would never hear Yeshua tell His own parables again. She had heard many of them secondhand, and they had blessed her. Still, she had hoped....

"He said the kingdom of God is like a mustard seed, which, even though it is smaller than all the other seeds, when it is sown upon the soil and grows up, it becomes larger than all the garden plants. It forms large branches so that the birds of the air can come and nest in its shade." Bilhah looked at Zlata, tenderness in her eyes. "The point of the story is that the kingdom of God may have had what seems an unimportant beginning—a carpenter from Nazareth and His unimpressive disciples—but the day will come when the kingdom's true greatness will be seen by all the world."

Zlata nodded, feeling some of the ache in her heart lessen.

"But He also used the mustard seed to teach us about faith. Even if our faith is that small, as tiny as that seed, it is still enough that we can say to a mountain, 'Move from here to there,' and it will move. Nothing is impossible for us if we have faith." Bilhah took hold of Zlata's hand and squeezed gently. "Have faith, my friend. As futile as the world looks today, I don't believe it will remain so. I don't know what God means to do. I don't know what will become of any of us. But I will hold on to hope. Yeshua gave me that hope. I will hold on to it." With a sigh, she rose from the bench. "I must see if Martha needs me." Then she walked back to the house.

A mustard seed. Zlata mused on the two stories Bilhah had shared. The parables seemed to say it was acceptable to have small beginnings in faith, in seeing the kingdom of God here on earth. Perhaps the need to forgive Taneli could begin small too.

Closing her eyes, she prayed softly, "Our Father who is in heaven, hallowed be Your name. Your kingdom come. Your will be done, on earth as it is in heaven."

It didn't seem to her that God's will was done on earth. Could it have been the Father's will that Yeshua was tortured and died on that cross?

And yet, Your will be done.

"Give us this day our daily bread."

She considered how the grinding of grain and the baking of bread was a daily routine. Like her ancestors of old who had gathered only enough manna for that day's journey in the wilderness, she was to trust her heavenly Father to provide for her on a daily basis. Even if she was alone. Even when she was afraid.

"And forgive us our debts, as we also have forgiven our debtors."

She pictured her father-in-law in her mind, his angry face, his raging eyes, even his hand raised against her. The image brought fear with it, but she didn't allow it to stop her.

I forgive you, Taneli.

She didn't feel forgiveness. She was still afraid. But it was a beginning. A small beginning.

"And do not lead us into temptation, but deliver us from evil. For Yours is the kingdom and the power and the glory forever. Amen."

Yes, His was the kingdom and His was the power and the glory. Somehow she would remember that in the days to come.

CHAPTER THIRTY-FIVE

Early in the morning on the first day of the week, Zlata and Bilhah set out on the road from Bethany, planning to visit the tomb where Yeshua had been laid.

"Others will be there before us," Bilhah told Zlata as they hurried toward the city.

The hated tears returned to Zlata's eyes again. She despised knowing Yeshua's body hadn't been properly prepared by those who loved Him best. He'd endured scourging. He'd endured being spat upon and mocked. He'd endured hours of hanging on a cross. Then, because of nightfall and the beginning of the Sabbath, his burial had been rushed.

They were drawing close to the Mount of Olives when they saw two men running their way. Bilhah took hold of Zlata's wrist and drew her to the side of the road, lest they be in the men's way. But one of them slowed, and Zlata saw that it was Joel. She hadn't seen him since the day of the crucifixion. She didn't know if he'd returned to the vineyard or if he'd stayed somewhere in Jerusalem. Everything that happened after Yeshua had been lowered from the cross was lost in a fog of sorrow.

Joel came to a stop, but the other man kept on running. Panting, Joel bent forward at the waist, resting his hands above his knees. Then he straightened again, and said, "He is risen."

"What?" Zlata and Bilhah responded at the same time.

"The tomb is…empty."

"Yeshua was taken?"

"No." Joel shook his head, still trying to catch his breath. "No, Mary of Magdala saw Him. He spoke to her and to the women with her. He called her by name and sent her to the twelve." He gasped for air a few more times before adding, "He said to tell them that He ascends to His Father and to our Father, and His God and our God."

"He lives?" Zlata whispered, almost as breathless as Joel.

"He lives." He said the words with confidence, and his face broke into a smile. "He lives, Zlata. The Master lives."

"He lives," she echoed, this time with more assurance.

Without forethought, she embraced Joel, pressing her cheek against his chest, almost laughing in her joy. He hesitated only a moment before his arms wrapped around her, and he drew her even closer, his chin resting on the top of her head. She allowed herself to remain there for a long while. Longer than modesty and tradition allowed. Long enough to realize what she had begun to hope for but didn't yet have the courage to grasp hold of.

She drew back and looked into Joel's familiar, dear face, regret coursing through her. If only she could say yes to him. If only fear didn't still hold her heart captive. If only…

Joel nodded once, as if he understood. Then he looked toward Bilhah. "Come. I know where to take you so you can hear for yourself."

Pilgrims no longer poured into the city. Instead, they poured out, returning to their own cities and villages, some even to other nations, now that the Passover and the Sabbath were over. Joel, Zlata, and Bilhah moved against the tide. They held on to one another so they wouldn't become separated. It was impossible to hold a conversation above the din. Each was left to his or her own thoughts.

Once away from the Temple Mount, the streets weren't as congested or noisy. Joel glanced over at the two women. "I'm taking you to the home of Kayin. He is a follower of the Master and can be trusted. Zebedee and Salome stayed with him for the Passover."

"They are here?" Zlata asked. "Zebedee and Salome? In Jerusalem?"

He gave a quick nod. "They arrived just before Passover. Salome was with Mary and the others at the tomb this morning."

Before Joel could say anything else, the sound of fast-moving feet reached them. He drew the two women quickly up against a building, pressing outstretched arms against them. Seconds later, Roman soldiers appeared around a corner. The sight of them jogging past Zlata struck terror in her heart.

After the soldiers turned another corner, the sound of them fading away, Joel said, "Come. We should hurry. The Romans must know by now about the empty tomb. There may be more trouble."

Zlata nodded and the three of them set off in silence again.

They found Zebedee, Salome, and Kayin in an upper room. Mary Magdalene wasn't with them. After hasty greetings all around, Joel told them about the soldiers they had seen in the street.

Zebedee said, "James and John. Simon. All the others. They're in hiding. Yeshua's resurrection has been reported to the high priests. Those in authority will not let this rest."

Salome touched her husband's shoulder. "Yeshua told us not to be afraid. This morning, when we saw Him, He told us not to fear." She looked from Zebedee to the others. "He said to take word to His brethren that they should leave for Galilee, and He would meet them there. Mary took the word to them."

"You saw Him?" Zlata asked breathlessly. "Yeshua."

Salome's smile was serene. "I saw Him."

"The Romans will want to find His closest disciples," Joel said in a grave voice. "So will the chief priests."

"For now, they are safe." Zebedee exchanged a look with his wife. "And you should all go home. Go home and wait."

"Wait for what?" Joel asked.

Zebedee shook his head. "I'm not sure. But I believe we will know. We will all know, each of us in our own time."

Silence filled the room.

Finally, Joel looked at Zlata. "I'll take you and Bilhah back to Bethany."

Go home and wait.

Zlata's emotions warred within her. Joy over Yeshua's resurrection. Fear because of the Romans and religious leaders. Uncertainty. Confusion.

Adonai, what do we do now?

Go home and wait.

PART IV

Spring, days after the resurrection

Then He opened their minds to understand the scriptures, and He said to them, "Thus it is written, that the Christ would suffer and rise again from the dead the third day, and that repentance for forgiveness of sins would be proclaimed in His name to all the nations, beginning from Jerusalem. You are witnesses of these things. And behold, I am sending forth the promise of My Father upon you; but you are to stay in the city until you are clothed with power from on high."

—Luke 24:45–49, NASB

Therefore many other signs Jesus also performed in the presence of the disciples, which are not written in this book; but these have been written so that you may believe that Jesus is the Christ, the Son of God; and that believing you may have life in His name.

—John 20:30–31, NASB

CHAPTER THIRTY-SIX

A few days later, early in the morning, Zlata left the home of Mary and Martha. She hadn't slept well since the crucifixion. Even the knowledge that Yeshua lived wasn't enough to bring peace back to the nights. She had slept little the previous night, great joy mingling with deep sorrow, and so she went to be alone and to pray.

As daylight began to fall over the land, she walked along the still quiet road. She didn't have a destination in mind until she realized she had come to the Mount of Olives. This was where the Lord had come to pray the night of His arrest. He'd known what lay ahead of Him. He'd told His disciples in advance of that night. And so He had come here to pray.

"So will I," she whispered, tears blurring her eyes as she sank to her knees. "Lord, if only I could have seen You one more time."

Her words were selfish, but they were honest. She couldn't help but think them. If she and Bilhah had left Bethany earlier on that morning, they might have been with Mary and Salome and the others when they went to the tomb. They might have seen Yeshua, walking and talking.

"I wish I could have been one of them."

Yeshua's disciples had seen Him later that same day. Lazarus had brought the story from Jerusalem two days later. How Yeshua had appeared to the disciples out of nowhere in the room where they had gathered. How He'd shown them the wounds in His hands and His side. How the ten men had been amazed by and rejoiced in His presence. How Yeshua had told them, "Peace be with you; as the Father has sent Me, I also send you." Then He'd breathed on them and said, "Receive the Holy Spirit."

"Thomas," Lazarus had added, "the one also called Didymus, can't make himself believe them since he wasn't there. He swears that unless he sees the Master's hands and can put his finger into the place of the nails he will not believe."

Zlata brushed away the tears on her cheeks. "Thomas is wrong, Lord, not to believe. I know it is true. I know You have risen, that You live. Still, I wish that I hadn't missed You when You spoke to the women. I could have been there. If Bilhah and I had left Bethany earlier that morning—" Her pitiful prayer broke on a sob.

"Why do you weep, My daughter?"

Zlata gasped in surprise as she looked up.

For a moment, she didn't recognize Yeshua, even though He stood near enough to see His face clearly. He was the same but not the same. "Lord?" The word came out on a breath.

"Zlata, others have looked for Me in an empty tomb. You looked here…and found Me."

"I came here to pray."

He smiled tenderly. "And found Me."

"I found You." The tears returned to her eyes and fell freely down her cheeks.

Yeshua moved to sit on a large stone, some distance still between them. Zlata wished she could sit beside Him, the way she'd seen some of His disciples do when He was teaching. She wished she could wash His feet with her tears as she'd seen Bilhah do and anoint His head with costly perfume as she'd seen Mary do. But an invisible hand kept her on her knees.

"Master," she said, "will You stay in Jerusalem?"

"For only a short while."

"Master, will I…will I see You again?"

"Not in the way you mean, My daughter." The tender look remained on His beloved face.

"Why?" she whispered.

"I go to prepare a place for you. If I go and prepare a place for you, I will come again and receive you to Myself, that where I am, there you may be also."

A place for me. The words stirred something inside her. For so many years, she hadn't had a home to call her own. There'd been no real place for her in the midst of Taneli's household. But the Messiah Himself would now prepare a place for her. She would never be without a place again.

"After a little while the world will no longer see Me, but you will see Me; because I live, you will live also."

Zlata bowed low, her forehead touching the ground. "Lord. Lord." Her tears dampened the earth beneath her. "Lord," she whispered one more time. Then she straightened.

But Yeshua was gone. As suddenly as He had come, He'd departed. And yet…Zlata didn't feel alone.

"I go to prepare a place for you.… I will come again.… Because I live, you will live also."

Zlata stood and turned in a slow circle, looking up through the tree branches that swayed in a cool morning breeze.

I'm not alone and…and I'm not afraid. She smiled in wonder.

"I'm unafraid," she said to the breeze. Then louder, "I'm unafraid!" She laughed, then turned toward the road. "I must tell Joel."

She ran then, as fast as her legs would carry her, toward Bethany, toward Joel, toward her future.

EPILOGUE

Two years later…

Zlata climbed the hillside, her right hand carrying a basket of fruit, goat cheese, and bread, her left hand resting on her extended belly. A golden hue blanketed the vineyard at this hour, and it was beautiful.

There were times when Zlata missed being able to turn her head and see the lake. For nearly thirty years, that had often been her view. But she had grown to love this rugged land too. Grapes grew best when they had to struggle, her husband of almost two years had told her.

At last she caught sight of Joel up ahead. She called to him and waved. He stopped in his work and waved back.

"I brought you something to eat," she said as she drew closer.

"You spoil me, my beloved. I could wait until evening."

"I know. But I wanted to do it. After the baby arrives, it won't be so easy for me to leave the house and come to you whenever I choose."

Joel reached out and covered her hand on her belly with his own. "After the baby arrives." Then he kissed her.

Delicious sensations sluiced through her at the touch of his lips. She loved him so. Such a blessing.

He led her to some shade and helped ease her to the ground. Then he sat beside her and, after thanking God, began to eat the food she'd brought him. Happiness flowed through her, and she marveled at how her life had changed, how the world had changed.

After the resurrection, Yeshua had appeared to many of His followers over the next forty days. Then, on the appointed day at the appointed time, Yeshua had ascended to His Father. Simon, who was said to have denied Yeshua three times on the night of His trial, had become the leader of the church in Jerusalem. He preached boldly and with great wisdom. Wisdom beyond that of a simple fisherman from Galilee. Numbers upon numbers of believers had been added to the ranks of those who knew Yeshua as their Messiah.

"You have that dreamy look again," Joel said, drawing Zlata back to the present.

She laughed. It amazed her how easily she laughed these days. "I'm just happy."

"I'm glad." He leaned close and kissed her cheek. "Of everything I want, your happiness is the most important of all."

"Ah, so it is *you* who spoils *me*."

He grinned.

"Joel! Zlata!" Matthias's voice carried up the hillside.

Zlata looked and saw the vineyard owner with his wife, Naomi, walking toward them. They were another blessing in her life. The two of them had become like parents to both Zlata and Joel.

"Look who is here." Matthias stepped to one side. Bilhah and Martha were right behind the older couple.

Zlata released a sound of delight. Months ago, she would have jumped up and run to them. Such a thing was no longer possible. Lately she couldn't rise from the sleeping mat without help.

Joel knew what she wanted. He rose then helped her to her feet so she could hug her friends when they reached her.

"We have come to be with you," Martha said. "We know your time is near."

Zlata's hand returned to her belly. "I hope so. I barely remember what it's like to draw an easy breath."

Bilhah laid her hand against Zlata's face. "And yet how happy you look."

"I am happy, my friend."

Zlata looked at the people surrounding her. Bilhah and Martha, who had become like sisters. Matthias and Naomi, who had become like a father and mother. Joel, the man she had disliked, then befriended, then trusted, then loved.

Thank You, Adonai. Thank You for bringing them all into my life. I am rich beyond imagination.

She thought of those two small copper coins, coins she had kept hidden for almost ten years. She recalled the sound they'd made as she dropped them into an offering box. She remembered the fear in her heart and the weakness in her legs.

She had learned, much later, how Yeshua called His disciples to Him that day and said, "Truly I say to you, this poor widow put in more than all the contributors to the treasury; for they all put in out of their surplus, but she, out of her poverty, put in all she owned, all she had to live on."

As always, Yeshua had looked at her and truly seen her. She smiled, this time through tears.

I am rich beyond measure.

She slipped her left hand into the right hand of her husband, and together with those who loved her, she headed down the hillside…unafraid.

AUTHOR'S NOTE

The Bible gives us only two pieces of information about the woman whom Jesus pointed out in the temple for her generosity: she was a widow, and she was poor.

As I pondered her, I realized that I'd always imagined her as old. But what if she was a young widow? How did that change her story? And what if she gave everything, not out of duty but because of her own encounters with the Living Christ? With those thoughts in mind, Zlata came to life in my mind and heart.

I've been writing Christian fiction for many years, and scripture has been a part of every one of those stories, just as it is a part of my personal story. But I have never been as immersed in the Gospels and the story of Jesus as I was throughout the writing of *Rich Beyond Measure*. It was a gift that I didn't expect when I agreed to write one of the Ordinary Women of the Bible novels. It is a gift I will always treasure. Thanks for joining me on this journey.

Robin Lee Hatcher

FACTS BEHIND

the Fiction

❖

WHAT WAS THE WIDOW'S MITE?

Jesus at the Jerusalem temple didn't see a widow donate two copper coins called "mites." Nobody called them that for centuries. The New Testament, written in Greek—the international language of the day—calls them by their Greek name: *lepta*.

Experts in ancient coins say the widow might not have donated two lepta. They say the Gospel writers, writing in Greek, may have simply used the Greek word for the smallest coin. She might have donated Jewish-minted currency such as the *prutah* or half-prutah minted during the Jewish reign of the Maccabees or in the days of Roman occupation, when Herod I and his son Archelaus minted coins that priests would have considered acceptable for the temple, since they depicted no people or animals.

THE ANCHOR/STAR PRUTAH OF ALEXANDER JANNAEUS IS TRADITIONALLY CONSIDERED THE BIBLICAL WIDOW'S MITE

The King James Version of the Bible, translated around the time of Shakespeare in the 1600s, first used the word "mite" for this coin. Readers at the time knew a mite was nearly worthless. Today, we could convey the value of the widow's donation by calling it a couple of half-penny coins.

HEROD I "THE GREAT" (40-4 BCE) ISSUED THIS PRUTAH. EXPERTS BELIEVE THAT MANY EXAMPLES OF THIS TYPE OF COIN CIRCULATED DURING JESUS' LIFETIME

Two lepta equaled the smallest Roman coin, called a *quadrans*. It would take 124 lepta to pay someone for a day's work. In Roman currency, that would equal a Roman denarius. So, out of an eight-hour workday, two lepta would have paid for less than ten minutes.

THIS PRUTAH OF THE PROCURATOR VALERIUS GRATUS WAS STRUCK IN 24 AD, NOT LONG BEFORE THE WIDOW'S OFFERING. IT IS ANOTHER POSSIBILITY FOR THE WIDOW'S MITE

HOW JEWISH LEADERS CHEATED WIDOWS

When a widow needed help settling her husband's estate, she turned to a scribe the way we would turn to an estate lawyer today. Sadly, Jesus said, some Jewish lawyers of the time helped themselves to widows' estates. "They cheat widows out of their homes" (Luke 20:47 CEV).

A JEWISH SCRIBE FROM AROUND THE TIME OF JESUS

Scribes weren't just secretaries who could write. New Testament writers portray them as legal experts who knew the Jewish law well enough to handle legal matters and write contracts, loan agreements, and wills.

When some husbands wrote wills to protect their family, they assigned a specific scribe to manage the distribution of their estate. When the husband died, if he had a young son, the scribe would appoint a guardian to manage the estate until the boy grew up. Or the scribe would manage the estate himself. He would do the same for a widow without children—for a fee.

Scribes could easily exploit widows in many ways. They could:

- charge excessive fees for handling distribution of the estate
- serve as guardian over the estate, charging fees so high the widow eventually had nothing left but her home
- accept the house as collateral for legal fees the scribe knew the widow would probably never be able to pay
- instead of charging money, freeload by continuing to accept the widow's gifts of money and other assets
- charge the widow for intercessory prayer she requested on behalf of her family

Jesus said scribes who cheat widows "try to make themselves look good by saying long prayers" (Mark 12:40 NCV). He added, "They will receive a greater punishment."

Money usually changed hands when couples got married in Bible times. If not money, then assets or services of some sort were exchanged. These took one of two primary forms.

BRIDE PRICE

One was called a bride price. This was a gift the groom or the groom's family gave to the bride's father. It was a thank-you for the bride and at least a token payment recognizing the bride's value to her family. They lost a worker when she left. (In some parts of the world, this practice continues today.)

THE OLDEST KNOWN JEWISH MARRIAGE CONTRACT (449 BC), WRITTEN IN ARAMAIC, A LANGUAGE JESUS SPOKE

Jacob, father of twelve sons whose families grew to become the twelve tribes of Israel, had nothing to offer for Rachel. So he made a deal with her father, Laban. "If you will let me marry Rachel, I'll work seven years for you" (Genesis 29:18 CEV).

Jacob ended up working fourteen years because Laban switched daughters at the wedding. Jacob woke up with Rachel's older sister, Leah. He renegotiated with his devious father-in-law, eventually getting two brides for the bride price of two.

At a time when women were perceived as a commodity, bride prices varied according to the perceived market value of women.

When Abraham sent his servant on the hunt for a bride for his forty-year-old son, Isaac, the servant loaded ten camels with supplies. He also took gifts of clothing, silver, and gold jewelry—enough to give for Isaac's future bride Rebekah and to her family (Genesis 24:53).

Women of higher status commanded a higher bride price.

DOWRY

Then there was a "dowry." This included money or assets, such as jewels or housewares that the bride's family gave to their daughter. Conversely, a dowry could also refer to gifts the groom or his family gave to the bride, like the gifts Abraham's servant gave to Rebekah.

Wedding gifts for the bride, including the dowry, were intended to help her set up housekeeping. Wealthy fathers who wanted to marry off a daughter sometimes gave her a huge dowry, to attract a future son-in-law.

The dowry belonged to the wife, though, not to the husband. If the couple divorced, she took the dowry, or an equivalent in value. At least, that's how it was supposed to work. Sometimes the dowry "disappeared," and the wife was left with nothing.

Women weren't allowed in the Jewish temple courtyard where priests sacrificed animals on the altar. That was a men's-only sacred space. Jewish women worshiped in the Women's Courtyard, just outside the Jewish Men's Courtyard.

Non-Jews—Gentiles—were banned from both Jewish courtyards. Engraved stones warned that if any Gentile stepped foot into the Jewish courtyards, he would "have no one but himself to blame for his death."

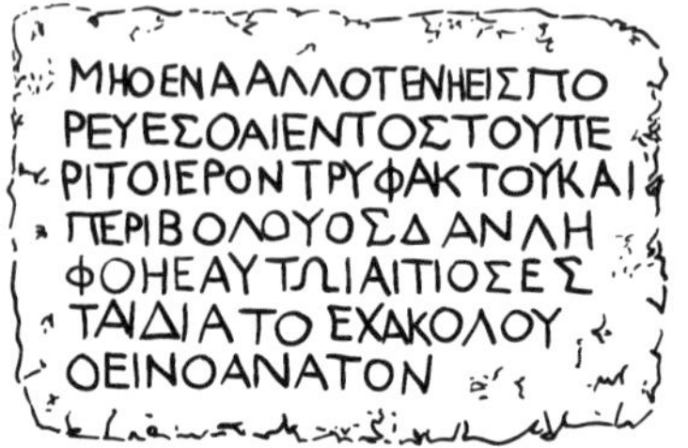

ENGRAVED STONE ON INNER WALL OF TEMPLE, WARNING GENTILES TO STAY OUT OR RISK DEATH. ONE OF THE STONES HAD TRACES OF RED COLORING IN THE LETTERS, SUGGESTING THE WARNING WAS POSTED IN RED. "NO FOREIGNER IS TO ENTER THE BARRIERS SURROUNDING THE SANCTUARY. HE WHO IS CAUGHT WILL HAVE HIMSELF TO BLAME FOR HIS DEATH WHICH WILL FOLLOW."

Gentiles worshiped in the sprawling and busy outer courtyard. This may have been where merchants rented space to sell priest-approved sacrificial animals and where bankers exchanged foreign currency for coins approved at the temple. Temple coins were forbidden to feature engravings of people or animals. "You shall not make for yourself an image in the form of anything in heaven above or on the earth beneath or in the waters below" (Exodus 20:4 NIV).

Jesus sometimes taught "in the place where the temple treasures were stored" (John 8:20 CEV), a space whose precise location we don't know. First-century Jewish historian Josephus (AD 37–100), born a few years after the crucifixion of Jesus, said Jews kept the treasure "in the inner court of the temple" (*History of the Jewish War* 5.20). If he meant the Men's Courtyard, women weren't allowed there.

But the Women's Courtyard was also one of the two interior courtyards walled off from the massive courtyard for non-Jews. Men had to pass through the Women's Courtyard to get to their courtyard with its sacrificial altar.

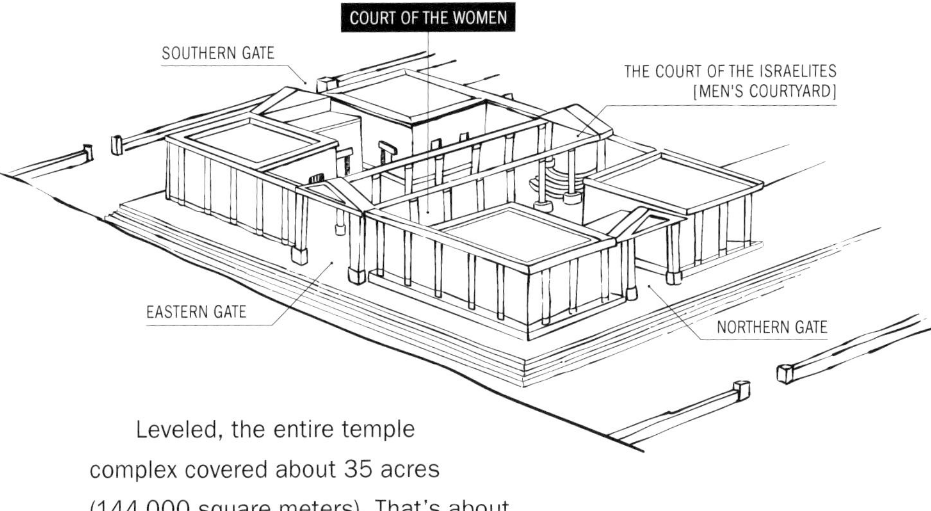

Leveled, the entire temple complex covered about 35 acres (144,000 square meters). That's about 29 football fields. The Women's Courtyard was a square 67 yards (62 m), a little more than one football field.

ASSETS FOR THE TEMPLE

Nothing in Jewish law demanded a penny offering. So scholars guess the widow's copper-coin offering was voluntary, not one of the required offerings.

MONEY FOR THE TEMPLE

Jews brought to the Jerusalem temple offerings of money and grain, along with animals for sacrifice. Meat left over after the rituals went to the priests, as part of their salary. They could eat it, sell it, or give it away.

On top of these offerings, Jews paid an annual temple tax of two drachmas for temple maintenance. That was two days' salary. Jesus arranged for a fish to pay his tax, along with Peter's (Matthew 17:27).

Most money for the temple came from tithes. "Ten percent of everything you harvest is holy and belongs to me, whether it grows in your fields or on your fruit trees" (Leviticus 27:30 CEV). Jews paid their tithe in produce and livestock or in equivalent currency.

ANIMALS AND CROPS FOR THE TEMPLE

Jewish worship included several kinds of sacrifices and offerings.

Burnt offerings. Usually, Jews killed and burned an entire goat or sheep. A rich person might sacrifice a bull. Poor folks sacrificed a bird. No one ate any part of this offering.

Sacrifices like these purified sinful worshipers. The animal's death substituted for the death the person deserved for sinning. God said, "Life is in the blood, and I have given you the blood of animals to sacrifice in place of your own" (Leviticus 17:11 CEV).

Guilt offerings. Worshipers sacrificed animals and followed detailed rituals for specific sins mentioned in the Jewish law—even unintentional sins. For example, if a person accidentally touched a ritually unclean animal such as a pig, these were his instructions: "You must confess what you have done. Then you must bring a female sheep or goat to me as the price for your sin. A priest will sacrifice the animal, and you will be forgiven" (Leviticus 5:5-6 CEV).

Grain offerings. Farmers brought grain, as kernels, flour, or even bread. Priests burned some as a thank-you to God. They kept or sold the rest as part of their salary.

Peace offerings. This is the opposite of a sin offering. It's a celebration and a big thank-you to God, expressed in the burning of part of a sacrificial animal. The worshipper would eat the rest, usually with family and friends.

LIMITED OPTIONS FOR BIBLE-TIME WIDOWS

A widow's best hope for a good life in Bible times, if she didn't have a son, was to find a brother-in-law willing to marry her.

Jewish law obligated the dead man's brother to marry the widow and give her a son to inherit the dead man's estate. "Their first son will be the legal son of the dead man" (Deuteronomy 25:6 CEV). This is called a Levirite marriage. In Latin, the language of the Romans, *levir* means "husband's brother." People in many cultures practiced this custom throughout the Middle East, Asia, and Africa.

If the widow couldn't find a willing brother-in-law, she could look for another male relative. Or any man. Or she could search for a scribe willing to serve as a paid guardian to manage her husband's estate for her, since she couldn't do it herself because she was a woman. Generally, women couldn't own property, and no bank would refinance her mortgage if she didn't have a guardian with her.

There were exceptions. Documents dating to Roman times report two Jewish women arguing over property. Other documents suggest Jewish women inherited property from their husbands as well as their mothers.

Information is sparse about what it was like to live as a Jewish widow, and how they survived. Ruth's widowed mother-in-law, Naomi, left what is now Jordan and moved back to Bethlehem to be with her relatives. Ruth joined her and married one of Naomi's relatives: King David's great-grandfather, Boaz.

And for those who had no other recourse, prostitution was an option of last resort.

By contrast, God's people were shown another way: "I am the Lord, so pay attention! You have been allowing people to cheat, rob, and take advantage of widows, orphans, and foreigners who live here... But now I command you to do what is right and see that justice is done. Rescue everyone who has suffered from injustice" (Jeremiah 22:2-3 CEV).

Jewish law ordered farmers to leave some of the harvest in the fields "for the poor, including foreigners, orphans, and widows." (Deuteronomy 24:19 CEV). Jesus's disciples assigned a team of seven men to distribute food to Jerusalem widows, which "pleased everyone" (Acts 6:5 CEV).

Justice and security for widows is a message Jewish leaders preached and practiced from the time Moses organized them into a nation until Jesus and the apostles, more than a thousand years later, began teaching that everyone should act like citizens of God's kingdom—and love and take care of one another.

Fiction Author
ROBIN LEE HATCHER

Robin Lee Hatcher is the author of over eighty novels and novellas with over five million copies of her books in print. She is known for her heartwarming and emotionally charged stories of faith, courage, and love. Her numerous awards include the RITA Award, the Carol Award, the Christy Award, the HOLT Medallion, the National Reader's Choice Award, and the Faith, Hope & Love Reader's Choice Award. Robin is also the recipient of prestigious Lifetime Achievement Awards from both American Christian Fiction Writers and Romance Writers of America.

When not writing, Robin enjoys being with her family (she's a mother of two, grandmother of six, and an "extremely young" great-grandmother of one), spending time in the beautiful Idaho outdoors, Bible art journaling, reading books that make her cry, watching romantic movies, and decorative planning. She makes her home on the outskirts of Boise, sharing it with a demanding papillon dog and a persnickety tuxedo cat.

Nonfiction Author

STEPHEN M. MILLER

Stephen M. Miller is an award-winning, bestselling Christian author of easy-reading books about the Bible and Christianity. His books have sold over 1.9 million copies and include *The Complete Guide to the Bible, Who's Who and Where's Where in the Bible,* and *How to Get Into the Bible.*

Miller lives in the suburbs of Kansas City with his wife, Linda, a registered nurse. They have two married children who live nearby.

*Read on for a sneak peek of another exciting story
in the Ordinary Women of the Bible series!*

THE LIFE GIVER: SHIPHRAH'S STORY

by Carole Towriss

Even whispers seemed too loud tonight. The whimper of a babe was quickly hushed by a mother who rocked the child, humming deep in her chest as the night grew darker outside, as the inhabitants of the little home and their guests waited. Waited. Waited.

The meal had been eaten. The bitterness of herbs still coated their tongues, and the smell of the charred remains remained heavy in the ash-laden air. But although their bellies were full of roast lamb and hastily prepared bread, the strangeness of the evening, with its blood-coated doorways and odd commands from a prince-turned-prophet, had made even the youngest of the children uneasy. As they should be.

"Why must I wear my sandals, Imma?" asked one girl, her wispy brows furrowed as she tugged at the new papyrus cord between her toes with a grimace.

"Hush," said her mother, smoothing a gentle palm over her child's busy hands to still them. "It is what we were told to do tonight."

"But why is tonight different than other nights?" she asked.

Her mother lifted her eyes and met those of her own mother beside her, helpless to explain to her child something she did not understand herself. The past few months of turmoil had been both frightening and hopeful, inexplicable and yet long-awaited.

Blood. Frogs. Lice. Flies. Livestock deaths. Boils. Hail and fire. Locusts. Three days of night. All of it had been terrifying and yet in His divine mercy, El Shaddai had laid a palm over His people, giving them a reprieve from many of the plagues that struck their masters. But tonight...tonight something dark hung in the air. Something far blacker and weightier than the darkness that had suffocated the land and shown the Egyptians that even their exalted god of the sun had no power.

"Tonight, my little rabbit," said the grandmother, answering for her daughter as she touched the girl's lightly freckled nose with a gentle finger, "is the end of this story, and the beginning of a new one."

"Which story?" asked the girl, leaning forward, her ebony eyes gleaming with anticipation for a story from the lips of her *savta*.

"Oh, one that began so very long ago. So far back that perhaps I do not even remember the beginning," she said, her lips curling into a coy smile as she tapped her chin.

"But you must!" said the girl, sliding from her mother's lap to her grandmother's. Her small hands gripped the woman's tunic, and she seemed to have forgotten the discomfort of her new sandals. "Please, Savta, I want to hear the story. What is it about?"

"Well," said Savta, "it is about you."

"Me?" repeated the girl, those dark eyes widening in disbelief. "How could a story so old be about me?"

"But it is," said her savta. "And also you"—she pointed to the girl's older sister nearby—"and you"—she gestured to one of her cousins—"and all of you." She spread her hands wide as she met the gaze of each child in the room, ever-so-skillfully ensnaring them, drawing them into the tale before she even began. She was widely known for her skill at weaving words into stories, accompanied by expressive voices and gestures that not only kept the children enthralled but somehow stitched together such a vivid tapestry of words that they were rarely forgotten.

Indeed the little girl's mother already knew which story would be told tonight. It was one she had heard many times over, one she could practically recite alongside her mother and one that she'd heard from the lips of her own savta many years before. And now it was time for her own daughter to learn the tale she would one day pass to her own granddaughter.

"There is a land called Midian, far, far away. Over desert sands and tall mountains and across a mighty stretch of water," said Savta. "And it was in this place of burning sun and fickle rains that a babe was born. Not in a home like this one, with mud-brick walls and a sturdy roof, but in a tent that shivered beneath a full moon as sandy winds tugged at its moorings with hot, insistent hands."

She paused, giving the children a few moments to follow her into the desert within their own minds. Already they were leaning forward, eyes fixed on their savta, the discomfort of sandals strapped on their feet and the eerie silence outside the little house overshadowed by the gently rising tone and soothing cadence of their grandmother's familiar voice.

"But the child was born too silent, too still, and the midwife's heart sank as she held the tiny girl in her capable hands, hands that had guided hundreds of babes into the world and seen almost as many delivered without the thrum of life within their chests."

"No," whispered one of the children, one who was well-acquainted with the sorrow of losing a sibling at birth.

Savta nodded sadly. "As all midwives know, death is ever hovering at the door as a mother labors, and only the Eternal One knows which babe will be spared and which taken. But as the midwife took in the tiny features of the little one cradled in her palms, dreading the moment she would have to tell its mother—her own daughter—of its passing, something deep inside told her that this was not the end, that this child would one day stand against the flow of a mighty river and not be moved. She knew that voice. She'd heard it speak to her before during particularly difficult births and trusted it, so she took the clean cloth that had been over her shoulder and began to rub the little one's body vigorously, whispering encouragement and willing the tiny lips to part and draw breath."

"Did they?" asked the freckle-nosed girl.

"They did," said her savta with a smile, and the children cheered the good news. "A great cry burst from her mouth and the midwife placed her upon her mother's breast with eyes full of tears and the knowledge that the Eternal One had a special purpose for her. But she also knew that it was not the end of this child's sufferings, not by any stretch of the imagination."

"What happened to her?" asked one of the boys, around the thumb he'd jammed in his mouth while his father and uncles had painted the blood around the doorposts of the house and had not removed since.

"For many years the midwife thought she might have been wrong, had perhaps misheard the voice that had whispered in her soul. But even so, she told the little girl the story of her birth time and again, reminding her granddaughter that death had hovered outside the door that night but that she had been spared for a reason. And then"—she paused again, meeting each child's gaze with deliberate intensity—"in the eleventh year of the girl's life, the river overflowed its banks, winding its way across the sands and tall mountains, over the mighty stretch of water and carried her away."

Gasps of shock rippled around the room as the savta waited, knowing that no longer were the children worried about the death that hovered at their own door tonight but were now completely engrossed in the tale.

"But fear not," she said, with a sly grin that slowly stretched across her face as she took in the aghast expressions of her grandchildren, "that is not the end of her story, but only the beginning…."

A NOTE FROM THE EDITORS

We hope you enjoyed another exciting volume in the Ordinary Women of the Bible series, published by Guideposts. For over seventy-five years, Guideposts, a nonprofit organization, has been driven by a vision of a world filled with hope. We aspire to be the voice of a trusted friend, a friend who makes you feel more hopeful and connected.

By making a purchase from Guideposts, you join our community in touching millions of lives, inspiring them to believe that all things are possible through faith, hope, and prayer. Your continued support allows us to provide uplifting resources to those in need. Whether through our communities, websites, apps, or publications, we inspire our audiences, bring them together, and comfort, uplift, entertain, and guide them. Visit us at guideposts.org to learn more.

We would love to hear from you. Write us at Guideposts, P.O. Box 5815, Harlan, Iowa 51593 or call us at (800) 932-2145. Did you love *Rich Beyond Measure: Zlata's Story*? Leave a review for this product on guideposts.org/shop. Your feedback helps others in our community find relevant products.

Find inspiration, find faith, find Guideposts.

Shop our best sellers and favorites at
guideposts.org/shop

Or scan the QR code to go directly to our Shop

Find more inspiring stories in these best-loved Guideposts fiction series!

Mysteries of Lancaster County

Follow the Classen sisters as they unravel clues and uncover hidden secrets in Mysteries of Lancaster County. As you get to know these women and their friends, you'll see how God brings each of them together for a fresh start in life.

Secrets of Wayfarers Inn

Retired schoolteachers find themselves owners of an old warehouse-turned-inn that is filled with hidden passages, buried secrets, and stunning surprises that will set them on a course to puzzling mysteries from the Underground Railroad.

Tearoom Mysteries Series

Mix one stately Victorian home, a charming lakeside town in Maine, and two adventurous cousins with a passion for tea and hospitality. Add a large scoop of intriguing mystery, and sprinkle generously with faith, family, and friends, and you have the recipe for *Tearoom Mysteries.*

Mysteries of Martha's Vineyard

Come to the shores of this quaint and historic island and dig in to a cozy mystery. When a recent widow inherits a lighthouse just off the coast of Massachusetts, she finds exciting adventures, new friends, and renewed hope.

To learn more about these books, visit Guideposts.org/Shop

Printed in the United States
by Baker & Taylor Publisher Services